The plot for this story developed over a twelve-year period as I engaged in a "truth quest" of my own—reading and researching several areas of science and technology to discover what they have to say about the existence of God and the makeup of the cosmos. My life's work in ministry and international missions has allowed me the opportunity to have extended conversations on these subjects with hundreds of brilliant and fascinating people from around the world—medical doctors, scientists, teachers, college professors, engineers, astronomers—and all have found amazing evidence that points to the existence of God. And while I have encountered numerous open-minded, honest people doing an awesome job of sorting through the quagmire in their personal search for truth, I realized that scientific truth is anything but unbiased. It is driven by philosophies, special-interest groups, political agendas, and religious dogma. Often I wondered if I might be able to weave this philosophical, social, and educational tension into a book.

My first attempt to write a book on this subject failed. It contained mere evidence, theory, and scientific data. I knew the challenge would be in how to present academically rich content in a way that would capture the imagination of readers while adequately addressing the battle for truth in our culture. Finally, I decided to write a science-fiction novel based on the many interesting people I have met in real life. For years, whenever I traveled, I dedicated any down time—on planes and trains or in hotels—to writing my story. After finishing the manuscript, it sat on my shelf for many years until one day I was asked by a publishing company if I had any finished manuscripts they could read to evaluate my writing. I laughed and replied, "I do have one old manuscript sitting on a shelf collecting dust." They encouraged me to send it in. To my surprise, they saw potential in it! Thanks to people like Terry Bailey and others at Innovo Publishing who edited and rearranged the manuscript, my book,

Truth Quest, became a reality. They have been very patient with my insane schedule, and I cannot thank them enough.

I need to include just one more note. Though I am now serving as a Representative in the Iowa State Legislature, this story was written several years prior to any thought I had of seeking a political office. I now find it humorous how well this story captures many of the dynamics of the real world of education and politics. —*T.B.*

TRUTH QUEST

Terry Baxter

innovo
PUBLISHING

Published by Innovo Publishing LLC
www.innovopublishing.com
1-888-546-2111

Providing Full-Service Publishing Services for
Christian Authors, Artists & Organizations: Hardbacks, Paperbacks,
eBooks, Audiobooks, Music & Film

TRUTH QUEST

ISBN: 978-1-61314-314-8

Cover Design & Interior Layout: Innovo Publishing LLC
Printed in the United States of America
U.S. Printing History

First Edition: February, 2017

┌─────────┐
│   │
│   1   │
│   │
└─────────┘

QUANTUM CONNECTION

Do romance and physics have anything in common? That sounds like a strange question until you consider that both can predict with a high degree of certainty what might otherwise be a totally unexpected outcome. For example, romance presumes that opposites attract. Likewise, the physics of quantum mechanics speculates that attracted opposites just might be the fabric that holds together the entire universe.

At their first meeting, Nick Davis and Brenda Randal stretched the definition of *opposites* right to the breaking point. Nick was from Iowa; Brenda, from Massachusetts. Nick was a product of the conservative Christian home-education movement; Brenda, the shining star of a very liberal private school for what some called "brilliant brats." Nick's parents had been married for over thirty years; Brenda's had just celebrated twenty-eight years as live-in "significant others" in an open relationship. Nick's father was a fundamentalist, pulpit-banging preacher and his mother, a stay-at-home mom homeschooling nine children; Brenda's father, on the other hand, was a fiery lawyer for the ACLU and her mother, the state head of Planned

Parenthood with national political aspirations. As far as opposites go, Nick and Brenda were not even from the same social galaxy.

In order to describe their first meeting, we need to take a trip back in time. Both were seniors in high school, and the event was the national high school science fair. The only thing these two had in common was a fascination with science, but even there they had totally different fields of interest.

Nick's project was an attempt to reconcile the new string theory of the cosmos with quantum mechanics and Einstein's calculations of both space and time warps. His research model confirmed the prediction that time manipulation was possible and even envisioned a mechanism to make it happen. His drawings included a test model similar to a giant atomic particle collider. Ideally, he envisioned two manned travel pods being launched from a space station and propelled through the universe by an initial-controlled nuclear fusion blast. This "controlled bang" would propel them in exact opposite directions at nearly the speed of light. Theoretically, one would move forward in time and the other backward in time. They would forever be acting upon one another, however, because of their common origin. It's a strange quirk predicted by quantum mechanics. His project not only caught the attention of the national education department because of his homeschool background but also raised eyebrows of physicists around the world.

Brenda, on the other hand, was fascinated with genetics. She was driven, in her own words, by "research that had some real humanitarian benefit." Her project proposed a way to repair the human genetic code of families who were at risk to pass on genetic susceptibility to diseases like cancer or diabetes. According to her project, live stem cells could be harvested from a human host and then genetically modified. These modified cells would then be cloned into live human embryos, which would have the exact genetics as the host. The major benefit, however, was that the genetic flaw would be permanently corrected and even modified to include other desirable traits. These modified stem cells could then be harvested from an embryo in abundance and either injected back into the host for medical treatment or saved for fertilization for offspring reproduction. She argued that it was much more efficient to repair a few cells and use them to reproduce or clone many healthy cells than it was to attempt the tedious work of repairing many individual cells to use for direct treatment. An added benefit, she proposed, was that organ cells could potentially be harvested from the embryo and used to repair damaged organs in the human host. Her project not only raised eyebrows in the medical community but created a firestorm from science and ethical watch groups.

The science fair sparked an explosion between these two brilliant young minds and sent them at light speed in exact opposite directions. It came to a head when their parents got into a heated shouting match on the final day of the competition. Nick's father shouted to the judges in protest that Brenda's project was "an ethical and sinful disgrace from the pit of hell" and that it had "no place in a high school science competition." With many supporters in his corner, he led a protest to disqualify the entry from competition. To his surprise, however, the protest had the exact opposite effect and only attracted more attention to her project.

Not to be outdone by a "country hick preacher," Brenda's father called the media and publicly threatened a lawsuit from the ACLU if the judges at the competition even hinted that his daughter's entry wasn't viable. Within hours, members of the media had gathered, and the newswires were buzzing across the country with the story. This kind of stuff makes for good media drama.

Unfortunately, the actions of the parents put the outcome of the science fair in the realm of politics rather than academics. If truth be known, much of science is driven by politics rather than unbiased research and facts. The competition was settled with a split decision, or at least that's what the judges said. For the first time in history, the national high school science fair ended in a tie for first place. Nick Davis and Brenda Randal stood side by side on the same stage for a photo op. With the bright flash of the last camera they were propelled in exact opposite directions. Little did they realize that their lives and destinies were now forever connected by this common launch into scientific academia.

Nick was offered a full-ride scholarship to seven of the most prestigious universities in the United States. He settled on Texas A & M University. He set out to complete his undergraduate work in less than three years. This was no small accomplishment considering his career goal required not only a major in nuclear physics but also an advanced degree in engineering. He had reason to believe that his project would put him at the helm of both research and technical mechanical design. He was betting everything that his theory and design would actually work. He had no idea how he would finance his future project, but he knew his first step included a stellar education.

During that time, he was also able to refine his theory and work out key differences between his model of time manipulation and the standard notion of time travel. His theory of time manipulation involved artificially creating and then traveling down a space and time warp. Einstein had mathematically proposed the concept of space and time warps but did not have the technology to test or utilize it. Nick's model would effectively result in a compression of earth time and a decompression of warp time. The fixed orbit of a time pod would create its own time continuum. Both the speed and size of the orbit could be adjusted to manipulate time in any conceivable direction. In this way, the old adage, "I just wish we had more time," would actually be possible.

The benefits and applications of time manipulation were truly astounding. They could prove crucial for urgent scientific experiments. For example, a new drug or treatment for a worldwide epidemic could be developed, tested, perfected, and even mass-produced by scientists in the time warp. They could put five to ten years of work into a cure that would be ready for distribution within two weeks of elapsed Standard Earth Time. It would be possible to program the size of the space and time warp orbit to provide whatever time compression or decompression was needed by the project being undertaken. In theory, it was also possible to stretch time the other way. Those inside the capsule could experience two weeks of elapsed time while several years of Standard Earth Time (SET) would pass. The possibilities were endless.

Going backward in time would also be possible, but Nick argued that the standard concept of time travel was much more random and even haphazard. He viewed the danger of tampering with history to be more than what fallen human nature could resist. Such scenarios have been the subject of countless science fiction books and movies. In fact, it was the constant comparison of his model of time manipulation with the usual science fiction notion of time travel that made his work so frustrating.

Nick managed to finish his double undergraduate majors in physics and engineering in less than three years. By all standards, his academic achievements surpassed those of his classmates and skewed every bell curve. Several textbook publishers faced massive revisions following his detailed analysis of the text. He had trained himself to be detail conscious. Finding and correcting textbook flaws, especially mathematical equations in the seldom used homework section of the textbooks, became an amusing pastime.

However, one issue constantly nagged him during his years of undergraduate work. Try as he may, he could not escape the frequently asked question, Whatever happened to Brenda Randal? Though he had not heard much about her and had consciously tried to put her out of his mind, he couldn't forget that crazy incident back at the high school science fair. Maybe it was simply not knowing whose project actually won, or maybe it was something more, but her shadow hung over his academic career like a thick fog. There was an invisible link, or force, between them that could not be denied. It haunted him. It never went away.

2

GIANT COLLIDER

The academic achievements of Nick Davis eclipsed all but a few celebrated scientists, past or present. He was definitely not a pushover, and he was determined to prove his theories with a working model. He was driven by a sense of destiny. He had become a rising star in the scientific community and was being watched very closely by many people. Some of those people were good; many were not.

When he was in his second year of graduate school, Nick received a visit from two official-looking men. They had been hanging around the campus for several weeks and were never far from eyeshot of Nick. Rumor had it they were part of a new kind of campus security to screen out extremists before they could pull off an attack on campus. Most students laughed at the notion that Nick could be a security risk, but they had to agree that he was certainly cut from a different cloth. Though much of it was motivated by jealousy, many students began viewing Nick with suspicion. People around campus were uneasy.

Finally the eventful day came when the two men approached Nick and flashed their badges at him as they literally pushed him into an empty room. The timing was perfect, and no one on campus noticed the incident. During the private meeting that followed, they presented official government papers to validate both their identities and intent. According to their story, they were working for a special branch of the government that fit loosely between the defense department, government contracts, and cutting-edge scientific research. Even their explanation was obscured with jargon and secrecy. They then explained that the purpose of their meeting was to offer Nick an unprecedented half-billion-dollar government research grant to incorporate his time manipulation experiment into a giant nuclear collider secretly being constructed at a remote government research center in Arizona. Of course the offer was verbal, so no paper trail would be left behind if he refused. Also, as far as they were concerned, the meeting never took place.

The grant was tempting, but the offer came with some disturbing "fine print." In fact, it had quite a few serious and perplexing strings attached. First, all of the work conducted at the research facility was stamped "top-secret" as was his grant offer. Second, he couldn't consult or tell his parents, friends, or campus faculty about the offer. Third, the official position of the United States government was to deny that any plans or projects existed to build a giant nuclear collider. Finally, as far as the public record, the research center itself didn't exist. It was beyond the scope of public scrutiny.

Nick was not considered politically astute, but he intuitively recognized that "top-secret" had some interesting connotations and twists. For example, he guessed the guiding ethics of this particular facility bordered on illegal and that government regulations or restraints, depending on how they are viewed, wouldn't apply. Regulations were made for the general public and private sector. But because this facility technically didn't exist, how could regulations apply? It wasn't on the radar screen of any watchdog groups. He wondered if the "top-secret" status translated to experimental freedom or academic slavery for those who signed on the dotted line. A wrestling match unfolded in his mind.

On the flip side, he also realized that the research lab, equipment, and staff would be second to none in the world. If he ever wanted the chance to test his theory with a real working model, this would be his greatest and possibly only opportunity. Mathematical calculation and technical drawings can stimulate the imagination, but only a real test model could validate his theory. After ten years of devoted research and calculations, he yearned for more than drawings. He was driven to turn his detailed blueprints into concrete, steel, and microcircuits.

For the first time in over a decade, he also recognized that some of the greatest scientific minds in the Western world had not only noticed his work but also had cast their vote in favor of his model. The government takes calculated risks, but it doesn't gamble with this kind of cash. In graduate school Nick's ideas and model had brought more than a few chuckles from students and staff alike, but this unsolicited grant offer was no laughing matter. He was finally being affirmed! Someone believed in him! He now realized that he was on to something big—something really big.

The completion of the massive project was still several years out, but the grant ensured that he would have significant input into the design and construction of the project. Technically, he would be modifying an existing project rather than starting from scratch. He was told that it was just easier and more cost effective to consolidate two projects than to undertake separate experiments. He was also informed that timing was of the essence because of the work already undertaken on the giant nuclear collider. The window of opportunity to consolidate the two experiments was closing quickly. He recognized that it was now or never.

Nick was relieved to get this offer from the United States government. Ever since that bizarre science fair in high school, strange things had been happening to him. For some time, he had had the nagging feeling that his theory and ongoing research were being monitored by undesirable groups around the world. Security firewalls on his personal computers were continuously being breached, so he had made a strict practice of keeping all of his personal research and files on a dedicated and sanitized computer that he never connected to the Internet. Strange phone calls and generous travel offers to destinations in former Soviet bloc countries were constantly coming his way. Though flattering, the offers always left him unsettled. He always felt like he was being followed. He needed peace of mind. He wanted the games to end. Even though he had suspicions and distrust, and even though it meant dropping out of public and private contact for several years, he was ready to sign on the dotted line.

At first it proved a bit tricky explaining to his parents why they couldn't have direct contact except for a few approved holiday visits each year, but a bogus government post office box in California made sending and receiving mail easy, and his parents became too preoccupied with children and grandchildren to squabble about his infrequent trips home. The government also provided a fully furnished apartment in a quaint California town close to Silicon Valley for the few occasions when he needed to entertain his parents or a few close friends. Of course, those were the only times he would actually live there, but appearance goes a long way in establishing reality for unsuspecting people. He felt bad about the charade, but it was a small price to pay for the opportunity to live his dream and to make his mark in the scientific community.

Nick worked directly under the supervision of renowned physicist, Dr. Julie Summers, head of the entire research facility. Nick didn't know it, but work at the facility included much more than research in physics. For the first three years, the rest of the facility remained a mystery to him. It was not that it was off-limits; it was just that he was extremely focused, spending every waking hour on completing the giant nuclear collider and time manipulation tunnels.

Construction in the facility afforded Nick the opportunity to use experimental equipment not yet being used for real-world application. For example, there was a giant drilling machine that could bore a precision tunnel through solid rock, leaving behind a glass-lined tunnel with no burdensome rock residue; everything was melted right into the thick wall of the tunnel. Progress was slow by some standards, but the resulting tunnel was perfect— and for this project it had to be perfect; the smallest imperfection could spell disaster.

Over time, Nick and Dr. Summers talked about many subjects both from a professional and personal standpoint. Over the first three years, she explored his views on every branch of science, ethics, politics, economics, and even his personal theology. Technically, he was her understudy, but she methodically analyzed everything about him. She left no past experience or thought unexplored. He really liked her and, had she been fifteen years younger, he would have found her very appealing.

Although there was mutual respect and trust between Nick and Dr. Summers, and although every conversation was conducted in a professional manner, one thing bothered him. She had an almost unsuspecting way of asking all the questions, which put him in the place of doing most of the talking. She would often wax eloquent in areas of technical science but was amazingly silent about her own past and about her personal views in less definitive areas such as ethics. He was transparent with her, but she remained a mystery to him. She knew him better than he knew himself, but he sometimes wondered about her true identity and full role at the facility. Was she a scientist, psychologist, or secret agent? One thing he knew for sure: she was both real and mysterious at the same time.

The day came when Dr. Summers decided to form a special oversight committee comprised of the supervisors of each facility department. As Nick walked into the conference room, he was amazed at the number of people who headed departments. Most were obvious intellectual nerds who, because of their preoccupation with experiments they had reluctantly left for this untimely meeting, paid little attention to others in the room.

The introductions were straightforward and to the point. "This is Dr. Anderson; he is supervisor of the experimental chemistry department. This is Dr. Davis; he supervises the experimental atomic physics department." His introduction was foreign to his own ears. He was still rehearsing it in his mind when he was hit with a lightning bolt. "And finally," said Dr. Summers, "this is Dr. Randal. She is supervisor of the experimental genetics department."

Nick quickly looked in her direction; she was already staring at him. She was dressed in a modified surgical gown and cap. He wasn't sure if it was Brenda. Besides, it had been over ten years since they had stood for that photo op together. Nick felt his face turning red. That was a new feeling for him. Was it anger, shame, joy, or what? He wasn't good at interpreting his own emotions.

Altogether there were more than fifty people in the room, and all Nick could think about was Dr. Randal. Their eyes met several times during the meeting. Was it her? And if it was her, what kind of top-secret experiments might she be supervising? Science has the potential for so much good, but it also has the potential for incalculable evil. What else might be happening in this facility? What could an experimental chemistry department be working on? Suddenly his mind was racing out of control. What had he gotten himself into? For the first time he began to have doubts about the facility and his involvement. His heart sank, and he felt sick to his stomach.

As she closed the meeting, Dr. Summers announced, "I would appreciate it if Dr. Davis and Dr. Randal would remain with me for a few moments after the meeting."

Emptying the room must have gone quickly, but it seemed like an eternity. For some reason, both now tried desperately to avoid eye contact.

When the door closed, Dr. Summers broke the silence. "Well, Dr. Davis and Dr. Randal," she paused, "or should I say Nick and Brenda? I think you two have met before."

That's all it took for words to start flying. It was an awkward moment, and neither was prepared for the shock. It had been ten years, but when emotional dams break, innocent bystanders can be swept away in the flood. This was the first time Dr. Summers had witnessed either of them come close to an emotional edge.

Fortunately, Dr. Summers didn't need any help saving the meeting. She spoke with piercing authority. "I want both of you to be silent and hear me out!" With that command, they snapped to attention. "I know there is bad blood between the two of you, but I want to remind you that you are now professional scientists, and your past is ancient history."

With that statement, they both began to blush. She was right, as usual. The only acceptable response at the moment was a silent mouth and listening ears. Dr. Summers had become a trusted mentor to both of them. She was usually all ears and encouraged open dialogue; however, this was not one of those times. They could sense that she was about to share something very important, personal, and even private.

She continued, "You both have worked here now for several years and have done an outstanding job in your respective fields. No one in this facility knows what I'm about to share with you, and I trust that this conversation will remain exclusively between the three of us." A moment of silence preceded the next words. "I have been diagnosed with—" She paused to control her emotions. "Let me just say, a medical condition." The words hit both of them like a freight train. "I have devoted my entire life to science. I have never married or pursued a serious relationship." She broke into a smile. "Contrary to popular opinion around here, I do think about those things, and I do have emotions. I just have never met a man who ignites fireworks in my heart."

Nick and Brenda exchanged a quick glance and chuckle. Dr. Summers had been the subject of numerous jokes and locker room conversations at the facility. But there was a greater irony in her confession. The students, judges, parents, and media at that crazy science fair a decade earlier would never have guessed, but the sparks between Nick and Brenda had been caused by more than just jealousy and anger. They themselves denied it, but for some reason neither of them had dated seriously since then.

Dr. Summers continued. "I have decided to start training two supervisors as my facility assistants. They will work together very closely, and the three of us will become a facility management team. When I'm away having treatments or taking time out to recuperate, these assistants will have to carry the entire load. They will be expected to communicate very closely with me, of course." She looked at both of them with piercing eyes. "The two whom I select will have to carry the load of their own departments, plus be cross-trained to supervise every other department. Let me get to the point. If the two of you think you can put the past behind you, I have decided that you are the best choices for the job."

Brenda spoke first, "Well, with the security around here, at least our parents will never find out." Then with a smile she added, "If my dad knew where I was working, he would sue the whole federal government."

Nick laughed and said, "Yeah, and just think of what my parents would do if they knew we were working at the same facility." That brought a roar from both of them.

Dr. Summers looked a little puzzled. Was she observing progress, or had she missed something in all her years of exploring the depths of these two young professionals? "There's one catch," she interrupted. "I know both of you have very different value systems and convictions. Nick, you believe in a personal God, and Brenda, at best, I would describe you as agnostic. The two of you have very different ideas of right and wrong. Nick, you believe in absolutes while Brenda sincerely believes that good ends justify questionable means. Believe it or not, I consciously try to balance both of these views in my approach to science, especially when managing a facility like this. We may have more latitude around here, but that's no excuse to throw caution to the wind."

Nick breathed a very obvious sigh of relief. She continued. "There is a lot of tension in the realm of science, and I have to make some very difficult calls at this facility. The two of you can appreciate this tension more than most. From the time you developed your love for science and started following your dreams, you have grappled with critics and the pain of mischaracterization. The two of you have learned the value of respecting your critics and viewing your work through their eyes. Those in our field who fail to consider the inherent potential danger of their own work make very careless and dangerous scientists."

This was unlike any conversation Nick or Brenda had ever had with Dr. Summers. Her mask was coming off, and they were beginning to see the real person behind the mysterious name badge. For once, she was doing the talking and they were listening.

She continued to speak from her heart. "I have lost countless hours of sleep over the realization that many experiments being conducted in this facility have the power for great good or for great evil. Inside this facility is the power to save human civilization or to destroy life as we know it." She paused and then spoke with great clarity and authority. "May God help us to do right and not wrong."

Nick wondered if this was a confession of faith, a prayer of sorts, or just a philosophical statement of moral goodwill. Brenda was just as surprised to hear the woman she had grown to admire use the word *God* in such a reverent way.

Then came the climax of her proposal. "Should the two of you accept this offer, you can never, in my absence, grant permission for a new venture unless you both come to absolute agreement. That includes the first test of a new experimental technology. Do you understand?"

That brought a moment of silence and deep contemplation. They both knew reaching consensus would be difficult. The challenge of overseeing their respective departments was demanding enough. How would they handle the responsibility of the entire facility? For that matter, how had one woman gained the trust and respect of our national leaders to be solely entrusted with this kind of responsibility? Who was this amazing woman?

They realized they were in the presence of a national treasure. She was a human icon whose identity and service would never be known by the world she loved, protected, and sacrificially served. She was a true hero of humanity, and for the first time they had found someone both of their parents would admire.

"Take time to think this through individually and then meet and talk together." Dr. Summers concluded the proposition with one final twist. "If one of you decides not to take this position, you are both automatically dropped from consideration. There will be tension and disagreement between you, but the future of the world depends on that tension. I will expect your answer in one week."

3

UNCONTROLLED IMPLOSION

The research facility's accommodations rivaled those of a fine university. It was equipped with everything from weight training rooms, gymnasiums, an indoor swimming pool, and outdoor hiking trails to theaters and shops. There were even exotic restaurants besides the regular institutional dining room. All the accommodations and attractions were free for resident workers, but by far the biggest attractions were the library and the computer lab. People in the facility actually read technical journals for leisure—that is, when they were not writing or editing them.

There were no sports teams there because game schedules would be nearly impossible to coordinate. Highly regarded were those sports that fostered times of solitude, reflection, and problem solving. It was not uncommon to find abandoned sports equipment at the exact spot where a brilliant idea had occurred to a scientist dressed in sweatpants and tennis shoes. One man was known to have stood at a free-throw line on a basketball court for over two hours. He would dribble the ball a few times and then hold it as if in deep thought. He never did take a shot at the basket. At some point he just dropped the ball and walked off at a rapid pace to his laboratory.

Most of the people at the facility had a tragic lack of social skills. Some would walk around in deep contemplation, often talking to themselves. Others would converse with one another in technical terms that most lay people couldn't understand. Then right in the middle of a conversation one might say, "That's it!" then turn and walk away. It wouldn't offend the other person, for he would usually keep right on talking out loud for several minutes before he realized he was alone.

Normal sleeping and eating patterns did not exist. Researchers did not punch time clocks. They chased inspiration, working tirelessly on formulas and theories. This was partly why Nick and Brenda had worked at the same facility for so long but had not yet crossed paths. Actually, it was highly likely that their paths had indeed crossed, but professional focus explains why neither of them had noticed.

Three full days after Dr. Summers issued her proposal, Nick and Brenda met at 9:45 p.m. for dinner. It was kind of late in the evening for ordinary people to get started, but these two were definitely not ordinary people. They had decided to use this first meeting to catch up on the past twelve years and to relegate details of their respective experiments to subsequent meetings. As the meeting unfolded, they were cautious and protective. Professional trust came easy, but history took deliberate effort to navigate. It was evident that they both were very mature and composed compared to earlier years. They were even able to talk about very different convictions with mutual respect and emotional equilibrium. It was a good sign.

They would meet three more times over the next three days before deciding on an answer for Dr. Summers. They had much to wrestle with, along with some big surprises. One surprise was how often their sleep was interrupted by romantic thoughts of each other.

In their second meeting, Nick was pleased to discover that Brenda had modified her views on human cloning. Under her direction, the genetics department was in the early stages of doing genetic repair on human organ tissue that could be used to clone specific organs rather than entire human embryos. The new organ could then be used for transplant with zero percent rejection possibility. It would be a remarkable medical breakthrough that could bring hope to millions of people with terminal illness, and with no negative ethical ramifications. Nick could not have been more thrilled at this revelation. Brenda was actually moving toward a more conservative camp. Though it did not represent her personal convictions, it did show maturity and respect for her critics.

The third meeting drifted into a conversation about education, ethics, politics, and theology. Brenda still despised home education on the grounds of anti-socialization. Nick was still skeptical of political special-interest groups and held the ACLU in contempt. Brenda had concluded that a supreme being might exist but felt that "He" or "It" was at best mysterious and unknowable. Nick had decided to save his own personal testimony for a future meeting. They both agreed that care must be taken with scientific ethics but took totally different routes to arrive at that conclusion. The meeting ended with a tingle in both of them that usually didn't come from an ordinary meeting of professional minds.

The final meeting was about Nick and his duties at the research facility. Brenda had rightly predicted that he was still working on his time manipulation project. She confessed that she hadn't heard much talk about the project among her circle of colleagues at the facility and was very curious. However, she had failed to make an important connection. She was, in fact, aware of both the construction and the sharp controversy surrounding the giant nuclear collider but had no idea that the project included time manipulation tunnels nor that the project was under Nick's supervision. He could tell that the revelation touched a nerve with Brenda, but little did he know of the storm that awaited the two of them.

Some respected scientists at the facility had real concerns that the giant nuclear collider experiment could backfire and, in essence, undo the Big Bang. They reasoned that it could, in theory, become the catalyst to reverse the motion of the universe from expansion to contraction and ultimate collapse. If the giant collider walls were to fail to contain atomic collisions, they would melt and begin to enfold. Intense heat would instantaneously be generated, and an irreversible magnetic pull would be created. Shortly, the physical matter of planet Earth would begin to collapse into rapidly condensing matter. Once the process started, it would be impossible to stop. In short order, all the physical matter in our solar system, including the Sun, would be sucked into the enfolding whirlpool—a black hole—resembling the apocalyptic warnings in the book of Revelation.

Nick didn't know it, nor did Brenda tell him, but rumors of the near completion of the giant collider had resulted in the formation of a "secret society" within the research center whose immediate goal was to slow down progress on construction. To do this they needed to create internal interference with the project until outside influences could stop the completion and the inevitable first test of the giant collider. Their ultimate goal was to cause the entire collider project to be scrapped. One devious member of the group had even plotted to leak some slightly exaggerated but highly inflammatory information to an outside contact.

As the meeting continued, Nick innocently expressed both excitement and frustration over his project. Brenda was pleased that he exhibited more excitement over the time manipulation aspect of the project than the actual nuclear collider. He was amazed at Brenda's exposition of the potential dangers of the giant nuclear collider experiment. She seemed unusually well informed for a geneticist. She was sincere in lamenting the fact that the two projects were intrinsically linked to each other.

His next confession met a stone heart even though, at least outwardly, she managed to fake a little sympathy. He shared his frustration over wrong materials showing up at the job site and careless damage to key components being caused by workers, creating costly delays. As she nodded in what he interpreted as sympathetic agreement, he never suspected that a significant cause of his frustration was sitting across the table from him!

An interesting irony was beginning to unfold. Some of the leading scientists in the world had just transferred scientific progress and their own destiny into the arena of public politics. The ramifications would be far reaching and would threaten the existence of the entire research facility.

An implosion was underway, but it was not in the suspect giant nuclear collider or in the micro realm of quantum mechanics. The collapse was developing in the much bigger, but less predictable, realm of people and politics. Can you imagine an inescapable and rapidly imploding black hole of human destiny sparked by the good intentions but sincere ignorance of the greatest minds in the world?

4

TOTAL MELTDOWN

News from the outside world seldom got much attention within the busy confines of the research center. It was readily available but deemed irrelevant by most of the staff. Besides, the vast majority of news from the outside world was dominated by sports.

The consensus at this facility was that the modern world has some important lessons to learn from the ancient Romans. Historically, whenever the appetite of a society was satisfied by sports, it was a sure indication of either decline or inoculation by a ruling elite. At this moment, however, Dr. Summers was thankful that the outside world was distracted by the fall football season. Even political activists have trouble competing with the hypnotic effect that sports has on the general population.

Most of the "news" didn't amount to much. The highly analytical minds within the facility lamented that journalists no longer report the news; they create the news. Each of the major news services spins stories to fit a certain biased or philosophical grid. The true story is obscured by endless commentary from so-called experts. It was offensive for everyone at the facility to watch news agencies interview actors from popular television programs as authorities on technical issues. Dr. Summers was appalled that the general public had become so gullible as to be spoon-fed and controlled by the media and political activists in Hollywood.

Viewing headline news was highly frustrating, especially during an election season. Watching several news sources report the same story in order to patch together the real story was mundane and time consuming, and few serious researchers could spare the time or mental distraction. However, one small, secret group at the facility was paying very close attention to what was happening in the outside world.

During the past five years, two influential figures in the outside world had risen to national prominence. They spoke for very different and very powerful segments of society and were always at odds. Activist leaders and special-interest groups have not only strange bedfellows but also very defined enemies. These two men were archrivals with bad blood between them and old scores to settle.

In a relatively short period of time, Reverend Richard Davis from the heartland state of Iowa had become the national spokesman for the CCWC (Conservative Christian Watch Coalition). The group basically had the ear of the Republicans and some moderate southern Democrats on Capitol Hill. It was not financed as well as rival groups, but it carried some real weight and could pack a hard political punch. Any candidate seeking public office from the conservative side of the aisle needed to be on friendly terms with the CCWC. Let's just say that Reverend Davis knew his way around Capitol Hill.

In the opposite corner was the new president of the ACLU (American Civil Liberties Union), a hard-hitting and sometimes ruthless attorney from the state of Massachusetts. Dr. Thomas Randal commanded respect from nearly every segment of society. He wasn't known for his outstanding ethics but was feared for his underhanded tactics. The ACLU controlled a lot of expendable capital and skillfully used the court system as a weapon against any adversary. Whether or not a case had merit, it would launch legal suits for political reasons. It understood that legal defense was not only expensive but effectively divided opponents' focus, energies, and resources on several fronts, and a divided foe was easier to conquer. It also had become the legal clearinghouse for many liberal special-interest groups. Every group from Planned Parenthood to PETA (People for the Ethical Treatment of Animals) worked closely with the ACLU.

That's why it was so unusual when a private e-mail from the office of the ACLU was received at the headquarters of the CCWC. It said simply:

Rev. Davis,

We have recently received what I believe is a credible tip from a confidential source. We have conclusive evidence that construction of a giant nuclear collider is nearing completion at a secret government installation in Arizona. Our concern is that this project has serious environmental ramifications. Of less interest to us, but we believe of great importance to you, is the fact that this project could also hold the final key to human cloning. I recognize this is an unusual proposition, but we may have urgent reasons to work together on this matter. Our source stresses that time is of the essence. If this matter fits your "watch grid," please contact me via e-mail to arrange a private meeting so we can discuss in more detail. This afternoon would be an advisable time for our first confidential meeting.

Thanks,
Dr. Thomas Randal

Animosity runs deep between these two organizations, so the e-mail caught the attention of everyone at CCWC headquarters. Reverend Davis was skeptical and already had a crazy schedule planned for the afternoon; however, his legal advisors pointed out that the gesture represented an occasion to at least open congenial communications. It was an acknowledgment of respect that might prove advantageous at some point in the future.

A critical lesson had been learned from the world of international politics. Even the United States and the former Soviet Union had recognized the need for a "hotline" of communication between the two world leaders. The two superpowers seldom agreed on mutual policy, but when they did come to a consensus, their objectives were assured.

Reverend Davis cleared his schedule knowing full well that the meeting would be awkward. The two leaders not only represented radically different social agendas, but also they still had vivid memories of the high school science fair more than a decade ago.

The meeting went surprisingly well, but they didn't waste any time on small talk. It's not that they weren't curious; they were just too proud, or maybe too hurt, to talk about Nick and Brenda. Neither wanted to be in the position of admitting that he really didn't know what his son or daughter was doing as a career. It was an unsettling realization for both of them.

However, the content of the meeting proved to be very enlightening and alarming. After reviewing the text of the "leaked information," their differences evaporated. A few pictures confirmed beyond any doubt that the giant underground nuclear collider existed and was nearing completion. The technical vocabulary and detailed explanation of the potential ramifications of a failed test removed any doubt that the informant was a scientist and that the breach of security was justified. Extreme measures would have to be taken to protect the informant, even though they didn't exactly know his true identity. Their actions needed to communicate complete trust and confidentiality.

Their afternoon meeting confirmed that they needed to set aside ideological differences and past hurts and work together.

The task at hand was paramount and would require the pooled resources, staff, contacts, and talents of both agencies. They agreed to immediately drop several pending lawsuits to free up additional revenue and personnel.

Evidence proved that the research facility was irresponsible and clearly out of control. They agreed that the information in front of them merited seeking permanent closure of the entire research facility. This would be their long-term goal. Their immediate, short-term objective would be to revoke the "top-secret" status of the facility. They knew political maneuvering very well and were masters of effective power plays.

In Washington it is standard political strategy to aim higher than the stated objective. This allows room for negotiation as well as mutual recognition, congratulations, and applause at resolution. At the end of the day, both sides look good in the eyes of the public. But more significantly, it allows public watchdogs an opportunity to hold the government accountable. The government has an innate spite for anyone who tries to make it accountable.

The two groups reasoned that their combined voice and political weight could grease the gears on Capitol Hill. To buy time, they decided on an initial plan of action that involved three steps. First, a statement of intent would be sent directly to the president's office with both of their signatures. They were confident this would at least get the attention of the White House staff. Second, they would call a joint news conference to alert the public of pending danger. This would be the first step in igniting the firestorm of public opinion needed to push reluctant senators toward their proposal. Third, they decided to "fire a shot over the bow" of the research center management by calling for a special investigation. This ploy usually resulted in administrative scrabbling and gridlock. They were desperate to buy time, and this was the best avenue available.

Their strategy came directly from the playbook of the ACLU, which had a proven track record. They were confident of success. And why shouldn't they be? The key players being assembled for this political maneuver represented the most capable all-stars ever unleashed on Capitol Hill. This was the first time they had spoken on any issue with a united voice. They were assured of immediate bipartisan support.

Neither of them knew it, but the sincere actions of these two parents had threatened the lifelong dreams and aspirations of their own children whom they deeply loved and admired. Soon it would be too late for even them to stop the implosion they were about to set in motion.

5

CONTAINMENT CONTINGENCY

The next day brought the inevitable meeting between Drs. Davis, Randal, and Summers. The meeting opened with congenial exchanges and a few minutes of small talk. In this case, the small talk led to a monumental disclosure. When casually asked about her health, Dr. Summers responded, "I had more conclusive tests this past week, and the diagnosis is not good. It is now confirmed that I'm in the middle stages of liver cancer."

Nick and Brenda exchanged glances. They were devastated. They understood the terminal nature of this diagnosis. However, Brenda understood the severity more than Nick. While in her junior year of college, she had watched her mother die of the same condition. That experience had been her single greatest motivation to sign on at the experimental research center.

Not to be distracted, Dr. Summers quickly turned the conversation to the task at hand. "I assume the two of you have had time to meet and discuss my proposal." They both nodded in affirmation. "Well then, let's get right to the point. What have you decided?"

Nick spoke up first. "I've taken time to really think this through. Dr. Randal and I have some real differences; however, I feel that our time together was sincere and very profitable. I'm ready to commit."

"Okay then, that's one vote." Then she looked at Brenda. "And what about you, Dr. Randal?"

She hung her head and spoke slowly. "We did have a great time, but I don't think it will work. My answer is no."

Nick couldn't believe what he was hearing. He looked at Brenda and asked why.

She didn't say a word until Dr. Summers looked her in the eye and emphatically demanded an explanation. Brenda had this strange feeling that Dr. Summers knew more than she was volunteering.

"Okay," she nearly shouted. "Nick, I didn't know that you were in charge of the giant nuclear collider. It's created a lot of controversy, and several scientists—" she paused, "including myself—have been working to hinder the progress."

Nick just hung his head in disbelief. Both women could sense his pain. "Well, that helps explain the past few months. At least in here you can no longer hide behind your father's subversive activities."

Dr. Summers just watched the interchange. "Nick," said Brenda, "there's one more thing you need to know."

"What's that?"

"I honestly do not know how it happened. I have my suspicions, but someone in here leaked a story about the giant nuclear collider to the headquarters of the ACLU. Knowing my dad, he is going to be on the warpath." She then added, "Nick, he has no idea that I work here."

Nick didn't say a word. He just sat in total silence. How could he trust her, or for that matter, work with her?

34

Dr. Summers broke the silence. "Okay, Dr. Randal, I'm still waiting for your real answer. What's it going to be?" Nick tried to interrupt, but Dr. Summers cut him short. "Dr. Davis, I already have your answer. I'm waiting for Dr. Randal to speak."

She lifted her head and said, "You mean you still want me to serve on your team after everything that has happened?"

Dr. Summers didn't say a word. She just held up a document intercepted two weeks earlier. It was the intelligence report of the security breach leaked to the ACLU headquarters.

"So," said Brenda, "you knew about my involvement in the secret society before you asked me to serve on your team? But why would you want me?"

"I want you two to listen very carefully. This place is not about conspiracy or politics; it is about balanced and responsible science. We have assembled the best scientific minds in the world, but that doesn't exempt us from making mistakes. Unfortunately, honest mistakes can be made in the realm of scientific experimentation that are potentially cataclysmic. The two of you represent our greatest safeguard against disaster. That's why I made it clear during our first meeting that in my absence no new ventures will be permitted and no existing projects will be tested without your mutual consent."

She paused. "There is one more thing you need to know. Our conversation here today is not entirely private." She then spoke the phrase, "Picture please," and one entire wall flicked on like a large movie screen in high definition. On the screen appeared the president of the United States, his national security advisor, and two other men.

The president interrupted the silence. "Dr. Davis and Dr. Randal, I want to thank you for your attendance at this meeting. As you know, we are in a precarious situation. Dr. Summers is very ill, and our entire research facility is in serious jeopardy. I have invited your fathers to this meeting to calm their suspicions that our work there is of the highest moral integrity. As of this moment, they both have top security clearance about the existence of your facility. They also have general knowledge that the overall facility conducts sensitive but very important experiments."

Neither father had seen his son or daughter for over four years, and both men were still in shock. They had just witnessed the full exchange between the three people in the room and knew it was not staged. They had hundreds of questions, but those questions would not be answered for a long time.

The president continued, "I need to now ask both of you if you are willing to work together under Dr. Summers' direct supervision according to the terms of our agreement. Could you answer loud and clear without divulging any sensitive information?"

The slight pause was followed by, "Dr. Davis, how do you answer?"

"My answer is yes, Mr. President."

"Dr. Randal," continued the president, "how do you answer?"

"Mr. President, my answer is also yes."

"Then as President of the United States of America, I thank both of you for your sacrifice and service to our country. Dr. Summers will orientate you on all remaining matters, and I will be talking to you both again in the very near future."

The president then spoke to the men surrounding him. "And now, gentlemen, have I managed to satisfy your concerns that our facility is of the highest moral integrity and has the greatest quality control in place?"

The answer from both men in unison was, "Yes, Mr. President." Neither man was known for his emotions or trust of other people, but at that moment they both had tears in their eyes, and the president had two new proponents for his program. A little mutual distrust can go a long way to ensure confidence.

The public news conference between the ACLU and the CCWC went forward as scheduled. The announcement of dropping all pending lawsuits between the two organizations made national news. In fact, it was headline news. That night, many commentators speculated on the reasons behind this huge event, but not a word was spoken about the alleged existence of a giant nuclear collider. That was, after all, top-secret information.

6

Bio Pods

Dr. Davis and Dr. Randal's new duties and responsibilities started immediately. For the next month, there was intense orientation on every department at the facility. This was an illuminating experience for both of them and included disclosure of some highly sensitive research of which not even the president or his joint chiefs of staff had detailed knowledge. They recognized that the nature of the information entrusted to them meant the rest of their lives would be lived out under scrutiny, protection, and seclusion.

Progress on the giant nuclear collider continued without a hitch, with emphasis being placed primarily on the time manipulation tunnels project since it was deemed less risky. The tunnels were 80 percent underground and formed an oblong circle of about two hundred miles in circumference. Two tunnels were constructed with one on top of the other. This would allow the pods to be fired from a launch station either individually or back to back in opposite directions. They would travel at the exact same speed in opposite directions with one in the top tunnel and one in the bottom. In theory, this would simulate opposite orbits at very high speeds. If the experiment was a success, each pod would travel its own separate time and space continuum with one pod moving forward in time and the other moving backward.

A portion of the tunnel was above ground. Two exposed parts of the loop could be removed to launch a single pod into space for a later test. A pod could be programmed to form any size orbit. The return leg of the orbit would not only bring the pod back to Earth, but it would actually loop through the tunnel before being hurled back into space. The orbit could also be programmed so that the pod would loop through the tunnel at precise intervals. This would create a much longer time and space warp for the pod than could be achieved on Earth or in the tunnel itself. The orbit could actually have a circumference of millions of miles. It was an ingenious design.

This would be the first real attempt to incorporate Einstein's theory of relative space and relative time into a functional time manipulation mechanism. Because the faster you accelerate, the less time it takes to travel a determined distance, it is possible to manipulate the speed of time and space. By adjusting the speed of the pod and the size of the orbit, years of earth time could pass for those in the pod while mere weeks expired on Earth. The opposite could also be achieved.

One regret Dr. Davis had was that over the past seven years at the facility he had been so preoccupied with the construction of the tunnels that he had not yet designed and built the pods. This would be his next goal, and he knew construction would take several years. You can imagine his surprise when on the final tour of orientation Dr. Summers led them through a large stainless steel door. Right in front of them were two identical pods near completion. Both he and Dr. Randal stood speechless. His original plans had been modified and slightly enlarged, but the pods still looked very much like his drawings.

The pods, each sixteen feet in diameter and seventy feet long to fit inside the tunnels, were equipped with everything imaginable and some things that were very unimaginable. Each had its own small nuclear reactor to generate electricity and to power an experimental gravity/antigravity propulsion unit. This had not been part of Dr. Davis' original design. He was familiar with the theory but unaware of any research to develop it into functional technology. The propulsion mechanism added huge potential to the pods and drastically reduced the amount of nuclear fusion blast needed to launch the pods into sustainable orbits. He was very impressed.

There were two floors inside the pods. The top floor had areas designated for living quarters and food storage. The lower included a complete research lab with state-of-the-art equipment. Nothing was left out of the laboratory, including genetic codes for every earthly life form, both living and extinct. The raw materials were there to clone everything from the simplest bacteria to the most complex form of life. Even Dr. Randal was impressed. These pods were more technologically advanced than her lab!

The two scientists realized that in this room and in these pods every department of the research center converged. It was like stepping back from a small workstation on an assembly line and seeing for the first time the whole process and the finished product. The pods were outfitted to duplicate the entire ecological system of planet Earth elsewhere in the universe. Even more sobering, they could regenerate the biosphere on Earth if the need ever materialized.

Experimental nutrition packs were condensed into pill-sized capsules so that when placed for thirty seconds in what resembled a microwave oven, a full meal would emerge. Granted, they did not taste like mom's home cooking, but they were more nutritious. Water would be recycled and gathered from special condensers that would collect hydrogen and oxygen atoms while traveling through cosmic gas clouds at nearly the speed of light.

Both Nick and Brenda spent long hours exploring the pods and catching up with technology. Walking through them was like stepping hundreds of years into the future. In these pods, science and science fiction came together to form a new reality. Brenda marveled at how the pods demonstrated the advances of evolution, but Nick strongly disagreed, arguing that the pods did not evolve at all; they were the result of years of research and development by the most intelligent minds ever assembled. What they were witnessing was not the result of random processes over time; rather, scientists had filled the role of an intelligent designer. His arguments were persuasive. Brenda had to concede. After all, she had unknowingly been a significant part of the design team.

Dr. Summers smiled at the tension between her two young colleagues. Though she seldom took sides, she did occasionally interject questions for them to ponder. "Suppose these two pods are one day called upon to restart the biosphere on Earth or to populate a new planet. Would the result be evolution or creation by intelligent design?" She continued. "I have read the biblical account of Creation numerous times from a purely scientific perspective, and I'm amazed that the Days of Creation outlined in the Bible represent the exact order and steps we would need to take in order to repopulate our planet or to generate life elsewhere in the universe." She paused for emphasis. "I have participated in countless think tanks here at the research center that tackled this issue. To our amazement, the solution almost always correlates exactly with the Genesis account, step for step." She then very thoughtfully mused, "I wonder how relatively uneducated men coming out of an evolutionary Stone Age understood these scientific dynamics? Could it be possible that the Bible is more than a fictitious religious book?"

This conversation from Dr. Summers represented new territory for both Nick and Brenda. Neither of them had ever heard her converse about biblical issues. Nick seized the opportunity and encouraged Dr. Summers to elaborate. He asked what exactly had been the problem or scenario presented to the think tank.

Dr. Summers explained. "We called it the Mars Proposition. The think tanks were presented with the task of establishing life on the red planet. Our challenge was to outline the steps necessary to accomplish that objective." She spoke fluently as they walked as if she had spent a lot of time pondering the subject. "It was amazing," she continued. "Every group arrived at almost the same solution. The first manned mission would be to build a biosphere on the surface of Mars that could support an atmosphere conducive to life. Next, a source of water and sunlight would have to be provided. Third, genetics would need to be introduced. This usually started with plants, including trees, and then some insects to provide pollination. Next, some animals, and then finally people could be introduced into the biosphere and live without external life support. It was absolutely astounding how the solution always followed the same basic order as the six Days of Creation outlined in the book of Genesis. Not one scientist over the many years of tackling the Mars Proposition ever suggested that we could introduce one single living cell and then abandon the project to time and random chance." After a moment of silence she added, "Working through the Mars Proposition is what set me on a path towards belief in God. Intelligent design and guidance seemed to be the only rational solution."

This informal conversation had a major impact on Brenda. Dr. Summers had become more than a mentor; she was a valued friend. Brenda could not sleep that night. She replayed the conversation in her mind over and over again. It had challenged her basic beliefs about origins. She could not argue with the astounding conclusions set forth by these scientists.

As Brenda lay in bed watching the hands of time click by, she was keenly aware that another clock was ticking as well. Dr.

Summers was running out of time, and without intervention she would not survive. A cure for liver cancer had been Brenda's life's ambition, and she was now more determined than ever to find a cure.

7

URGENT TRANSMISSION

As the days went by, Dr. Summer's health continued to deteriorate. She would sometimes slip away for several hours to rest. Maybe that's why neither Dr. Davis nor Dr. Randal noticed the strange activity on the afternoon of May 15.

Secret Service had intercepted another unauthorized message. Only this time it was not a breach of security from within the facility but rather a message from outside beamed into the facility via Dr. Summers' secured presidential frequency. It was addressed specifically to Dr. Summers, so she felt justified in keeping the message confidential. She was confused and half thought it was a practical joke.

> *Dr. Summers, this is Paul again. Since our last correspondence, Mother died of old age. I calculated her age at ninety-five Earth years when she died. I calculate my own age now at close to 69.3 years of orbit time, ten weeks SET. I went over her calculations and discovered the problem. Our orbit sent us on a transverse time orbit to Earth. In other words, we have been traveling backward in time exactly twelve years for every fourteen days of Earth time . . . most of . . . equipment . . . still functional.*

*I . . . think . . . cannot survive . . . orbit alone. . . . theoretically
have . . . food . . . My loneliness . . . I occupy . . . time . . . only
hope . . . you follow . . . detailed instructions . . . last message . . .*

That was it. The message broke up and then went silent. It was a mystery. Who was Paul? Why was the message so choppy, and why was it cut short? For some strange reason, it had been cut off in the same way as when a cell phone loses coverage. The whole message was transmitted in less than a millisecond. It seemed to correspond with a solar flare or, more precisely, a solar flash over the research facility.

Dr. Summers passed it off to security detail as a humorous coincidence; however, she was anything but humored. Her mind raced. She desperately needed more data. What was that strange solar flash? Why did it correspond exactly with the time the message was received? Only Nick, Brenda, and the president himself had clearance to use her presidential secured frequency to transmit a message. Had security been breached?

She read the message one more time, soaking in every detail. "SET" was the terminology Dr. Davis had introduced in his high school science project. It stood for Standard Earth Time. Other parts of the message also intrigued her: "…twelve years for every fourteen days of Earth time," "…backward in time," "…69.3 years of orbit time, ten weeks SET." The message was received at exactly 3:00 p.m. on May 15.

Whatever was happening sounded strangely similar to phenomena that was to accompany a test of one of the pods. A quick check confirmed that both pods were present and accounted for in the staging area, although one had been placed in the first tube to await a basic test within six months. Light bulbs began to go on in her mind as Dr. Summers grabbed her calculator. She closed her eyes momentarily to get mind control over her pain. She was slipping fast—very fast. Her doctors now gave her less than three months to live.

Nick and Brenda were pushing hard on several fronts. Brenda was racing against time trying to produce a new liver treatment for Dr. Summers. She didn't want to lose this very special woman. She needed more time, and she knew only too well that she was losing the race.

Meanwhile, another race was taking place. For the sake of scientific research, Dr. Summers had sacrificed relationships and any thought of having her own family. She was only forty-three years old, but now her life was slipping away, and she knew she had made a mistake. For a long time it had been evident to Dr. Summers that whenever Nick and Brenda were together, there were fireworks. One day, shortly after returning from a very painful treatment, she made them face the issue they both had avoided. She encouraged them to not make the same mistake she had made. She said, "My greatest desire before I die is to see you two get married. Life is too short to spend alone. You're both in your early thirties, and you need to think about these things." At that moment, she sounded less like a scientist and more like a mother.

Neither Nick nor Brenda protested. By now they knew each other very well. They were fully aware of their differences but worked well together. Nick was a Christian, and although Brenda had not yet taken that step, she was more open than ever. Nick continually prayed for her salvation. Their biggest difference was in their child-rearing philosophy. Brenda was adamant that if they ever had children, homeschooling would be out of the question. Their children would require the best private school in the country.

The two set a wedding date for July 15 in the hope that Dr. Summers could make the wedding. They decided to have two wedding celebrations—one with colleagues at the research facility and another with family and friends in their "front state" of California.

Dr. Summers continued to deteriorate quickly. However, on May 29, she collected all her strength and headed for her secure office. She wanted to witness this herself. Just as she expected, at exactly 3:00 p.m. there was another solar flash and subsequent message.

> *Dr. Summers, this is Paul again. Mother is now eighty-eight years old and very feeble. I do not think she has much time to live. I am now 57.3 years old. I am sure she will not survive the next orbit. She successfully completed the liver treatment and trained me on details of the surgery. You must prepare pod tunnel #2 to catch us for landing on June 13 at 3:00 p.m. Will be ready for emergency surgery. Do not go in for scheduled treatment . . . instead be in pod room . . . only hope . . . please be . . . Paul Davis . . . God bless!*

This time the message made much more sense and confirmed her suspicions. She knew exactly what was happening and the identity of Paul Davis. Science fiction was colliding with reality, and her own future was about to be rewritten. So many questions were spinning in her mind. *What is my right future if it hasn't actually happened yet? Can I stop what is about to happen since decisions and actions in the future have already put events into motion in the present?* At the same time, she knew the future had a way of unfolding on its own. They were in uncharted waters, and many mysteries would unfold in the next few months.

Dr. Summers did not let Nick or Brenda in on these communications. Her mind was quickly filling in the blanks, and her intimate knowledge of Nick and Brenda and their wedding plans provided all the missing pieces. A woman much younger than her in real life had already died of old age in the past. A baby was conceived, born, educated, and aged in an opposite time continuum to Earth in one of the pods. She wondered if his body could adjust to a forward time continuum, or would the shock cause sudden death if they intercepted the pod. Even worse, would he grow younger with each passing day of Standard Earth Time until he met himself at birth? More mind-boggling, what if all three pods ended up in the control room at the same time? New physical matter was about to be added to the universe. Would the matter in the two "same" pods be stable or explosive? At least two people were about to meet themselves in separate bodies in the present. One would see himself born; the other would see herself as an elderly woman with no understanding of who she was meeting. One thing Dr. Summers understood very well was that this was no time for her to give in to her liver disease and die. She had to hang on and remain at the helm for as long as she could.

Her mind was reeling with questions. She was so weak. Should she tell Nick and Brenda about the decisions they made in the future, or should she let an unwritten future unfold on its own? Technically, Dr. Summers understood that she was already living in the past, or these issues wouldn't even be a concern. Suddenly, the ramifications of the time manipulation experiment made the nuclear collider experiment look minor. Should she inform the president? Both the questions and the pain of her cancer were unbearable.

8

CODE 1 LOCKDOWN

This was no time for indecision. Dr. Summers immediately placed an urgent work order for tunnel #2 to be prepared to receive a pod. The antigravity mechanism had never been tested, but it had to work to perfection. Nick had all kinds of questions, but answers did not come easily. He wondered why he had been left out of the decision-making process concerning these new work orders.

Dr. Summers explained that receiving a pod had to be perfected before testing a launch, in the event that a test pod went backward rather than forward in time. Before anything happened to her, she wanted to make sure this final phase of the experiment was in place. She knew it was a lame excuse, but Nick accepted it without question. In fact, he was disappointed in himself that he had not caught such a simple but important detail. Thinking in terms of time and space warps is not natural. Many things are backwards to Earth reality.

Without hesitation, Nick established three shifts so work could proceed twenty-four hours a day. His immediate concern was to be as efficient as possible over the next two weeks. They could not afford delays or mistakes. Nick wondered what Dr. Summers knew that he and Brenda were totally oblivious about.

Work progressed without a hitch, and the receiving mechanism was in place three days ahead of schedule. However, Dr. Summers was deteriorating so quickly she could no longer walk without assistance. On June 10, she placed an order for a mechanical drive wheelchair, and on June 11, she made her usual rounds from the pilot seat of her new chair. The scientists at the research facility were not known to be sentimental or emotional, but many tears were shed that day in every department. The wheelchair was a statement that a woman everyone revered, loved, and trusted was giving up and preparing for her own death. It was obvious that she did not have much time.

For reasons known only to her, Dr. Summers had opted to skip her next medical treatment scheduled for June 12–14. Everyone had admired her courage in pushing right up to the end, but they viewed this as a sign that she did not think she had the strength to survive the treatment.

On the morning of June 12, Nick and Brenda had their first confidential meeting behind Dr. Summers' back to discuss whether or not she was still competent to make decisions at the facility. Though her mind was intact and sharper than ever, her body was obviously starting to shut down. Brenda had been through this before as she'd kept vigil at her mother's bedside. She knew it was only a matter of hours or days before Dr. Summers would slip into a coma and then be gone.

Brenda lamented the fact that she had let Dr. Summers down and lost the race to save her life. She closed her eyes, clinched her fists, and whispered quietly, "God, this is why it is so hard for me to believe in you. If you are there and you are loving, then why would you let this happen?"

Early on the morning of June 13, Dr. Summers called Nick and Brenda to her bedside. She was too weak to get herself out of bed and into the wheelchair. They sat in silence for several minutes. As usual, Dr. Summers spoke first. "I have called the two of you here to concede my authority over this research center and transfer all responsibility to you. I have been in communication with the president over the past month, and he fully concurs with my decision." She paused to gather her strength and then continued. "In doing this, I am making one final order that you must obey without question or hesitation." They both nodded, more out of respect than agreement.

Her next statement shocked both of them. "At exactly 12:00 noon, the control room for the pods will be evacuated of all personnel. At 1:00, I will be wheeled into the control room with the pods and left alone, no matter what my medical condition. All doors will be locked and sealed behind me. Under no circumstances is anyone to enter the control room for seventy-two hours."

Nick and Brenda just stared at each other. They both loved and admired Dr. Summers, and there was no way they were going to abandon her to face death alone. It was time to declare her unfit and overrule this order. Technically the facility was prepared for an emergency shutdown and had even held occasional drills to prepare for such an event. However, this was not a drill, and Dr. Summers could not be left alone in the control room and survive for three days.

Dr. Summers anticipated their objection and cut them short. She then handed them an envelope and said, "Enclosed is a signed order from the president of the United States. You have six hours to prepare for evacuation and lockdown. For the next three days, this facility is on a Code 1 Lockdown. At 2:30 p.m. this afternoon, every lab will be closed and locked. Facility staff will be restricted to housing, dining, and fitness areas." She paused. "I'm sorry, Nick and Brenda, but these orders include the two of you. This might be a good time to work on your wedding plans."

The orders were authentic and carried the full weight of the president of the United States. Special agents and armed security guards were already taking their posts around the facility. It was clear that this was not a drill.

Dr. Summers looked at Nick and said, "What are you waiting for? You have work to do." As he turned to leave, Dr. Summers simply said, "I know you both have many questions. I am just asking you to trust me." She then turned to Brenda and said, "For the next six hours, you will be my personal aide. Your job is to get me dressed and into the control room by 12:45 p.m. Even if I slip into a coma, you will leave me in the control room alone at 1:00 p.m. That is an order! Do you understand?"

The evacuation and lockdown proceeded as a normal drill. All faculty personnel followed procedures to the letter. In fact, most of the scientists and assistants thought it was a drill until they stepped out of their respective buildings and were met by an army of Secret Service agents and armed guards. To ensure the Code 1 Lockdown, Secret Service agents collected all security passes. This was an unprecedented event at the research facility. Being restricted to the housing, dining, and fitness areas had a built-in security measure. They were designed and built to withstand a nuclear attack.

Every mind at the research facility was trained for problem solving, and that included racing through every possible scenario. Speculations and rumors began to circulate among the staff. The most prevalent one was that the giant nuclear collider was undergoing an initial safety test, and the evacuation was simply precautionary. An independent and unbiased branch of the military was most likely conducting the test. The number of armed Special Forces added credence to this position.

A Code 1 Lockdown was designed not only for the safety of the staff but also for the total containment of any accidents, spills, or other unforeseen hazards of research. This included biological, chemical, and nuclear containment. Research carried on at this facility eclipsed any risk factor previously known. None at the facility wanted to verbalize this possibility, but it was in the back of everyone's minds that something might have gone wrong. Every precaution was followed meticulously at the facility, but the potential for human error or equipment failure was always present.

The early absence of Dr. Davis and Dr. Randal had cast suspicion on the nuclear and biogenetic departments. Both areas represented potentially devastating accidents that could require containment. Of course, with their recent promotions to the facility management team, their absence was explainable, especially if Dr. Summers had slipped into a coma. If that were the case, the facility may have been going through an honorary lockdown.

By 12:00 noon, the pod control room was totally evacuated with the exception of Dr. Davis. He was ensuring that all equipment was left in automatic control mode as ordered by the president. At exactly 12:45 p.m., Dr. Randal and Dr. Summers entered the control room. Nick was relieved to see Dr. Summers in control of her own wheelchair; however, it was obvious that she did not have the strength to walk. She was the only person who knew every switch, button, computer, and control panel in the massive room.

Nick suddenly arrived at a daunting conclusion: one person sitting at the master control station could easily operate the entire room. Pod #1 was loaded in tunnel #1 and technically ready for launch. Tunnel #2 was now fully ready to receive a pod. His mind started spinning with calculations. *Let's see, seventy-two hours is plenty of time for a pod to complete one orbit of* . . . He needed a calculator or, better yet, a computer, but the lockdown ensured that neither would be available to him for seventy-two hours.

His eyes met Brenda's. She had come to the same conclusion. They were now to the point in their relationship where they could read each other's thoughts. *How can we stop this?*

wondered Nick. Brenda's look was even more desperate. *Do we have the authority to defy a presidential executive order?*

Dr. Summers was not left out of the loop. She knew exactly what the two were thinking. Nick and Brenda quickly discovered that though her body was weak, she was in total control of all of her mental faculties. At exactly 12:58 p.m., two armed Secret Service agents entered the room and stood at attention. Dr. Summers acknowledged them and then turned to her two colleagues.

She said, "I want to apologize in advance for what is about to happen. These two men are here to escort the two of you to the containment area. I cannot risk your safety or well-being with the unknown. Hopefully, I will be able to explain everything in full detail in seventy-two hours. If I do not survive, you can access a full briefing with your security codes on my personal computer. I will only say that I am trying to contain something the two of you unwisely started after my death in the near future, and that is all I can say at this time." She paused. "Please pray for me. I am about to wrestle with many unknown mysteries of the cosmos." She paused for a moment and added, "The next seventy-two hours are crucial for the future of human civilization." She concluded by saying, "You have your orders!"

She nodded at the two Secret Service agents. They stepped forward and simply said, "Dr. Davis and Dr. Randal, please lead the way. This is a Code 1 Lockdown. This is not a drill." They both took one final look at Dr. Summers and stepped through the reinforced titanium doors that were overlaid with thick stainless steel. The core was made of special lead alloy. They were designed to withstand a minor nuclear blast at ground zero without leaking any radiation. Similar doors were located down the exit corridor to form expanding zones of containment. This precaution was to protect the outside world from any unforeseen, toxic, or dangerous event that might occur in the control room. No safeguard had been overlooked.

At exactly 1:00 p.m., all doors closed, and the control room automatically went into total containment lockdown. In seventy-two hours, if the internal equipment and emergency checks declared an all-clear, the room would automatically unlock allowing manual entrance of authorized personnel. If the equipment detected a problem, the room would remain sealed indefinitely and encase itself in glass with the aid of a small nuclear fusion bomb. With temperatures reaching close to 50,000 degrees, everything in the room, including the tunnels themselves, would become a thick and impenetrable glass-like tomb.

9

PANDEMONIUM PARADOX

As Dr. Davis and Dr. Randal were escorted into the containment area, every conversation ceased and every eye studied them for clues as to what was happening. There were none. They looked almost as perplexed as the others in the containment area. Apart from the two stone-faced secret agents, they were the only ones who knew Dr. Summers was very much alone in the master control room. They decided to downplay this information for the moment and share it only if disclosure deemed necessary.

It was awkward being restricted to the faculty containment area. This part of the facility was completely underground and designed for protection from both inside the control room as well as any external threats. Only the regular facility security knew its true underground depth. Every exit door opened into an elevator. The ride to the top took over a minute.

Instead of windows in the dining area, there were high-definition screens displaying the external campus. For some reason, Dr. Summers had overlooked the small detail of turning off the real-time, high-definition screens. The birds, rabbits, and occasional deer crossing the campus were soothing sights. This was the first time many of the faculty had taken the time to notice them.

Computer access was restricted during the seventy-two-hour lockdown, but security had decided to continue outside television coverage of sports and news. The security guards preferred sports channels while the scientists gravitated towards news. A few of the more informed faculty joined the guards in watching sports. Their excuse to colleagues for this obvious intellectual lapse was "having the Chicago Cubs in the playoffs is as rare as witnessing the birth of a supernova. It's a cosmic event!" That brought laughs from everyone.

Then the unexpected happened. At exactly 3:00 p.m., a bright solar flash nearly blinded those looking at the outdoor screens, and there was a strong impact tremor like one that accompanies an earthquake. Several people in the containment area were knocked to the ground. Dishes fell to the floor, and furniture vibrated about the room. Lights blinked on and off, and all screens went blank momentarily before coming back on. At first, there was concrete dust in the air, but the ventilation system quickly cleared it away.

Most of the faculty scientists had done some undergraduate work in geology. Some shouted that they were at the epicenter of an earthquake. Others countered that it felt more like ground zero of a nuclear blast. Even the Secret Service agents looked pale with concern. They needed information and data, and they needed it fast. Some stood to leave, but the guards stopped them. The commanding Secret Service agent barked a loud command. "Our orders are very clear. No faculty is allowed to leave this area or have access to any computers or equipment. Back to your seats! This is Code 1 Lockdown!"

Shortly, the television stations interrupted with a special report. As is usually the case, the media made things worse by scrambling to get the scoop on the story. The headlines read: "Unconfirmed reports of an earthquake in a remote area of

Arizona possibly caused by a meteorite or an incoming warhead. Stay tuned for more developments."

Of course it didn't help when the media dispatched helicopters to the site only to discover that a military no-fly zone was in effect. Military fighter planes were already patrolling the remote area, and helicopters and all civilian planes were being turned back or grounded. Every wacko and conspiracy theorist in the country was busy feeding the rumors and spinning a story.

Nick and Brenda began to whisper. "What do you think?" asked Brenda.

"Well, there are three or four potential scenarios," replied Nick. "It could have been a pod launch, landing, or explosion in the control room." He paused for a moment and added, "Or it could be a combination of a landing or launch with an explosion. This is new territory for all of us. Let's just hope Dr. Summers . . ." He became very quiet, realizing the severity of the situation and her fragile condition. He started over. "Let's just wait until the lockdown is over so we can assess the situation. In the meantime, let's work on panic control."

They knew they had their hands full.

***

Meanwhile, back in the control room, things were even more chaotic. The receiving tunnel had been closed with huge reinforced titanium and stainless steel doors specially designed to absorb the impact of a landing. The impact, though, was much more severe than anticipated. The shock wave shook the control room so violently that Dr. Summers' wheelchair flipped over, and she was knocked to the floor. Though she was still conscious, she simply did not have the strength to upright her chair, nor did she have the strength to pull herself up into a standing position to operate any of the controls.

She now lamented her decision to remove Nick and Brenda from the control room. She needed them desperately. Her protective instincts may have jeopardized the entire project. Why didn't she at least grant them access to the remote viewing control room? They could have put the system into override and manually manipulated the equipment from the safety of the remote room. It was no use; she had put too much faith in herself, and now she was helpless.

***

Back in their private quarters, Brenda confessed that she had never felt more useless or helpless. Nick responded that they did have one recourse. He spoke softly but firmly. "Remember the final words of Dr. Summers before we were escorted out of the control room?"

"Yes," said Brenda. "She asked us to pray for her."

Nick took her hand and bowed his head. "Dear God . . ." Brenda closed her eyes out of respect, but inwardly she was wondering if there was anyone there to listen.

***

As Dr. Summers lay on the floor, she was startled by a distinct sound. The controls in the room were switching to override. Someone had tapped into the system and was taking over the control room. Within minutes, the huge titanium and stainless steel doors of tunnel #2 opened, and the shining glow of a third pod illuminated the control room.

The next scene was pathetically comical. Two figures stumbled out of the pod. One was a middle-aged man; the other, an old woman. They staggered around as if drunk. Paul Davis and a very elderly Dr. Brenda Randal Davis were trying to adjust to something far more shocking than jet lag. Time itself had just reversed for them and started moving in the opposite direction.

Dr. Summers couldn't help but chuckle at the sight. Paul opened his mouth to speak for the first time to a human being other than his mother. "Hello. I assume you are Dr. Summers and are expecting us. Welcome to our surgery pod and your scheduled appointment. If you would please join us inside, we can begin." It took the three of them over ten minutes to get back into the pod. Once inside, Dr. Summers was relieved to see that everything was prepared for the experimental medical procedure.

As the aged Dr. Brenda Randal Davis looked into the eyes of a much younger Dr. Summers, she said, "My friend, I've been waiting a very long time for this moment to come back to me. I let you down the first time; I'm not going to let that happen again." She paused long enough to look Dr. Summers over and then very candidly confessed, "You look terrible! As long as we're at it, do you need any other new parts? We can make them up in a few minutes."

Dr. Summers smiled and said, "You're the expert now. Give me the best you've got, and add whatever you think is best for me!" That might have been a mistake.

The medical equipment and procedures were much more advanced than anything on Earth. Paul, who was actually the new expert, performed the surgery, and his mother watched. The entire procedure lasted a little more than three hours. It would have been much faster, but technically, most of the procedure was more like radical organ regeneration than transplant. Growing a new liver, kidneys, heart, and lungs based on Dr. Summers' unique DNA code took a little time. The organic matter had been developed and organically grown from her personal DNA code without the use of any cloned embryo. While he was at it, Paul decided to also replace Dr. Summers' female organs. At age twenty-six, she had elected to undergo radical "female" surgery to decrease her risk of genetically transmitted cancers that had plagued her family. Dr. Summers slept through the procedure, so she couldn't really object. Paul even cosmetically cleaned up a few old scars left over from previous surgeries and injuries. The amazing part of the surgery was that there were no incisions, and there was no chance of rejection.

Following the surgery, the three slept for eighteen hours straight. Dr. Summers woke first and, for the first time in many years, felt fantastic. She could walk well but had some muscle atrophy from having been nearly bedridden in recent weeks. It would take a while to get back into shape.

She stepped over to Paul's bedside and gazed at his peaceful face. When Paul opened his eyes, the most beautiful eyes were looking back at him. Uninhibited, and knowing painfully little about tact, he spoke the first thing that came to mind. "Dr. Summers, is this feeling I'm suddenly having what is commonly called 'falling in love'? I think I know how Adam must've felt when he woke up and saw Eve for the first time." Dr. Summers turned red, and her heart began to race. Paul leaned close and whispered in her ear. "I've read everything about you. By the look of things, I'd say you're experiencing those fireworks you've always longed for with a man." Dr. Summers wasn't accustomed to others knowing more about her than she knew about them. Apart from a few chopped-up electronic messages, this man was a total mystery.

For the first time in years, her emotions were trying to override her intellect. Suddenly, she began to wonder what other surgical procedures Paul might have thrown in. She stepped in front of a mirror and opened her gown. She was shocked! Her new figure was stunning, though admittedly exaggerated in certain areas. "Wow!" She stood staring at herself until she realized that hers were not the only eyes looking.

"So, how did I do?" he asked.

"Well, that depends on your objective. If you were trying to create a supermodel, I'd say you did great! But if you were trying to help a devoted scientist, I'd say you managed to create a lot of distraction."

"Well, Dr. Summers, or can I call you Julie?—" She hadn't been called that name in a long, long time. He didn't wait for an answer. "I think God originally designed us for both work and pleasure."

Neither of the two had ever experienced the pleasure side of the original God equation. But this was definitely not a time for pleasure! They had a lot of work to do and a lot of decisions to make over the next thirty-six hours. Fortunately for them, having an aged mother in the room helped them to maintain professionalism.

Dr. Summers attempted a redirect. "We have a lot of questions to answer about the stability of what is happening with the atomic matter in this room."

Paul reassured her. "Don't worry; I know what you're thinking. I've thoroughly studied all the computer files stored on board at the time of blastoff and the theoretical physics of that time."

She was transfixed.

He continued, "I've already worked out all the details of what I call The Conservation of Energy and Matter in Time Warps and Overlaps of Multidimensional Realities."

Dr. Summers interrupted him. "Would you repeat that very slowly?"

He just continued talking. "What's happening here may be unique to Earth reality, but it happens quite often and naturally in many parts of the cosmos." He rambled on as if talking about elementary physics. "Because space and time warps are naturally occurring phenomena within the universe, physical matter appears to be gained or lost, but from a cosmic perspective, it is actually only shifted. The universe is far more stable than was previously predicted and is constantly undergoing phenomena far more radical than time and space warps and reversals.

"By the way, sorry about making so many unauthorized changes to the pod. I had no choice but to make many radical and emergency modifications to this antique in order to accommodate the dynamics of inter-cosmic travel. It is obvious that scientists who spent their whole life grounded on Earth designed and built it. Did you know there are space warps out there that make it possible to transverse or skip entire regions of the universe in cosmic travel? They are transparent to vision until approached at nearly the speed of light. The laws of physics do some radical things at those speeds and in space warps. We once hit an elliptical warp at nearly the speed of light. Not all space and time warps are the same. Because the distance across condenses by a factor of over fifty, our speed technically remained the same, but in relation to the rest of the universe, it increased to fifty times light speed. Gas clouds take on the density of a liquid at those speeds. I'm sorry, but this thing wasn't designed for that kind of ride."

For the first time in her life, Dr. Summers was in a conversation that went way over her head. She was both fascinated and frustrated. To think that an eight-week-old human in SET had lost her in an intellectual cosmic cloud was hard to accept. On the other hand, in actual body time, growth, and development, he was approximately her age and had a universe of experience.

Her mind was beginning to wander. *Get a grip,* she told herself. Life was a lot less complicated without emotions or hormones. *But is that really life?* she suddenly asked herself. *Has my devotion to academics and science opened new worlds and experiences or locked out many precious age-old worlds of experience?* Her mind raced. *Why would a man with Paul's intellect, academic depth, and cosmic experience be more fascinated with romantic fireworks than expanding fields of knowledge?*

She reflected on her own request made just prior to surgery: "You're the expert now; give me the best you've got and add whatever you think is best for me!" *Wow! Why did he restore my figure instead of expanding my intellect or filling me with more knowledge?* She was confident there was subliminal meaning in this gesture. For the first time in years she began to cry, and for no apparent reason!

As she watched Paul and his aged mother, Dr. Summers began to sense their immense loneliness and emptiness, yet there was a peace and tranquility about them that she had never witnessed previously. After nearly forty-five years of being isolated in a totally sterile, academic environment, they were starved for balance in life. They had become masters in every field of knowledge, not out of desire but rather out of a quest for survival. Solitary confinement is cruel punishment for even the most prolific minds.

They had essentially downloaded everything from the computers into their minds and memory just to pass the time and attempt to medicate the void of loneliness. They knew everything that could be known about planet Earth but had been isolated from experiencing any of its wonders. Paul had conducted manifold experiments in the cosmos and meticulously written and recorded volumes of new theories and data in the area of intergalactic physics. He had recorded and downloaded mega-volumes of new data and pictures from their journeys through many sectors of the cosmos. His mother had educated and trained him well, despite her previous aversion to home education.

The aged Dr. Randal then did something totally out of character. She sat down and invited Dr. Summers to join her. Paul reclined next to them as if totally accustomed to the ritual. Brenda said, "Dr. Summers, it was not my knowledge or scientific background that helped us survive these years of confinement. It was my faith in and growing relationship with God. The universe truly is full of order, design, and beauty. As a young woman, I was impressed with how much I knew and had concluded that science confirmed the nonexistence of God. I used to worship human knowledge until I discovered it was a very small and constantly changing god. Many of my scientific theories have been falsified or drastically modified through this journey, but the basic premise of this little book has been validated beyond human explanation." She spoke with a conviction and firmness that had not been present in her younger days. The calculated and liberal-minded skeptic that Dr. Summers knew so well had been transformed into a different woman.

She then opened a very worn Bible to Psalm 19 and began reading: "The heavens are telling of the glory of God; and their expanse is declaring the work of His hands. Day to day pours forth speech, and night to night reveals knowledge. There is no speech, nor are there words; their voice is not heard."

When she closed the Bible and her eyes to pray, Dr. Summers could make out these words on the front of the worn cover: "Most Cherished of All Gifts on Our Wedding Day." Underneath, in smaller print, were the words: "From Your Loving and Faithful Husband, Nick Davis."

Dr. Summers had so many questions. She looked down at her own newly regenerated skin and then at the very mature and aged wrinkles of Dr. Brenda Randal Davis. She was now an elderly woman, but why? Wasn't it possible for her cell regeneration treatment to prevent, or at least to stop, the aging process? In the first message, Paul had said that his mother died of old age. Why would she choose aging and natural death above human remedy? Had the aged woman come to understand that there is an eternal reality that extends beyond this life? She seemed so peaceful and resolved to approach and pass through its doors.

10

MISGUIDED CALCULATIONS

Things were going much smoother inside the control room than back in the containment area. With the full backing of the Secret Service, Dr. Randal and Dr. Davis were attempting to turn a deteriorating situation into some form of order. Most people were looking to them for direction. Recognizing the enormity of intellectual capacity present, the two decided to direct everyone's attention and efforts towards developing a contingency plan for whatever awaited them. They had less than forty-eight hours to come up with something. They would give each department a few hours to propose a theory of what may have happened then they would lead a think tank comprised of top research scientists from each department in order to compare theories.

In preparation, Nick and Brenda privately reviewed the evidence they had, including the fact that Dr. Summers was alone in the control room prior to the impact—or whatever had happened. As they examined the sketchy information that was available, they concluded that Dr. Summers had most likely prepared to receive a pod from the future. The urgent work order in the past two weeks, the solar spike, and subsequent quake—all pointed towards that conclusion.

Nick and Brenda decided not to disclose to the group the details of their last conversation with Dr. Summers. She had said, "I am trying to contain something the two of you unwisely started after my death in the near future." This was the piece of the puzzle that completed the picture for Nick and Brenda.

They began the meeting with a brief overview of the work orders of the previous few weeks and mentioned that Dr. Summers' last order had been for her to be left alone in the control room. Everyone was aware of her volatile condition. They also mentioned the possibility that some kind of test may have been conducted on pod #1, or something may have entered the receiving tunnel.

When they opened the meeting for discussion, the staff geologist spoke first. "Assuming you are correct that an incoming object may have entered the receiving tunnel, I am not very optimistic. Seismographic readings reported over the television from New Mexico indicate any man-made object could not have survived impact." He paused. "The other very real possibility is that what we felt was a minor nuclear blast. The control center may already be entombed. The spike may have triggered the entombing process."

Nick was keenly aware of that possibility. He had helped design the containment system. The impact they felt may have been strong enough to trigger the automatic detonation and containment mechanism. It was also possible that the blast was from the detonation and not the impact of a pod.

Dr. Nelton, the research chemist, spoke next. "By the appearance of the solar spike—or whatever caused that flash—I am confident that heat inside the tunnel must have been intense. It is possible that every rubber, plastic, and lead component instantly vaporized. The resulting toxic gas would be lethal. If

Dr. Summers somehow survived the impact, she most likely died instantly from the heat and poisoned atmosphere."

Nick responded with composure even though his voice betrayed his remorseful emotions. "So far we have possible radiation from a nuclear blast and toxic fumes from incinerated components. Do we have other possibilities to consider?"

A relatively new scientist specializing in the field of astronomy spoke up. "There is always the potential of cosmic contamination. Technically, anything harmful would be burned up in the atmosphere, but something carried in the core of an incoming vessel might survive atmospheric heat and be released upon impact. The likelihood is small but very real. It is currently one of the models under consideration for how meteorites might carry organic matter throughout the universe. No matter what happens, we cannot unseal the control room without establishing a secondary seal zone and before the all-clear is given."

The epidemiologist then spoke. "That does raise the real possibility of foreign bacteria or viral contamination. A foreign agent vigorous enough to survive transport could flourish in Earth's environment. Once released, there is no telling what could happen, especially if it infects a host or mutates quickly. Caution is of utmost importance."

Dr. Randal cut in. "Your point is well taken, and that's why we need your input."

Dr. Davis quickly changed the subject to avoid hysteria. If these scientists started functioning in panic mode, the previous leak to the ACLU and resulting damage control might appear minor. There was always tension among the faculty because these people, more than any, knew the inherent danger of an unexpected and uncontained accident. At this moment, the situation was deteriorating rapidly, and neither Nick nor Brenda had the commanding presence or control that Dr. Summers had with this group.

Just then, a Secret Service agent interrupted and handed Dr. Davis a memo. He was very relieved at its content. It read: "Note: Military planes in the target area detect no radiation or visible damage at ground zero. All looks normal." Dr. Davis read the report to the members of the think tank. It did alleviate some of the anxiety, but several scientists expressed distrust of military technology and reputability. They believed the military's duty of protecting national interests undermined the credibility of the report. It was the stereotypical attitude of all present and generated no debate.

"Okay," said Nick, "I want each one of you to review your emergency response plans and follow them to the letter as soon as the Code 1 Lockdown comes to an end. First, conduct a fast but detailed assessment of your department. Second, one hour after the lockdown has lifted, every department head is to report to the briefing room for joint analysis. Third, I need a team of four volunteers to accompany Dr. Randal and myself to the pod control room. We will depart from the assessment briefing directly to the control room. I want radiation, biophysics, epidemiology, and technical engineering departments represented. If for any reason you cannot go yourself, appoint a knowledgeable and competent replacement from your department. This team will take every precaution and dress in biochemical and radiation response suits. As we enter the main corridor leading to the control room, we will seal doors 1, 4, and 5 behind us. This will effectively create three isolation zones."

A colleague interrupted Dr. Davis. "Do you think we should activate Operation Blue Code?" Operation Blue Code had been designed as a backup measure to kill and sanitize the control room in the event of any suspected contamination from invasive bacteria. The procedure involved flooding the room with antibacterial gas that effectively kills any organic cells in the area without harming equipment. Unfortunately, it would also kill any people in the room.

"We will keep that option open," replied Dr. Davis, "but I want to give Dr. Summers the benefit of the doubt that she may have survived the impact. She deserves at least that much." Nick was surprised at the vocal criticism and doubt evoked by his decision not to employ Operation Blue Code. Many felt that preserving the huge amount of research and development within the various departments of the facility was a greater priority than preserving the actual control station and existing pods. They could be replaced, but if the whole facility were jeopardized, all would be lost. It was a gamble Nick was willing to take, but the others were not on board with his assessment.

The old faction between conservative and liberal scientists still existed within the research facility, but with Nick and Brenda now working together, they had no way of monitoring what was happening within the secret society. Brenda was held in suspicion by the group and put on a blacklist. The key leader had been transferred while the remaining loyalists went underground. Both Drs. Davis and Randal knew the secret society still had the ability, connections, and resources to pull off covert activity, but up to this point it had not been viewed as a viable threat. Both Nick and Brenda were glad to have the Secret Service guards in place monitoring the situation.

The network news services were still leading with the story. With no official explanation of the phenomenon and the no-fly zone still being enforced, strange rumors had gained credence and even validation from self-appointed authorities. Public hysteria was feeding the media, which in turn became increasingly more irresponsible in its desperate search for information and desire to keep the story alive. After all, breaking news means big audiences, and that means big money. It also means job security and promotions. Human nature hasn't evolved over the past two thousand years. People are still willing to crucify truth on the cross of self-interest and profits.

11

FINAL DEBRIEFING

Paul spent the remaining time of Code 1 Lockdown trying to adjust to Standard Earth Time. It was not an easy process. Having lived his entire life inside the travel pod, he wasn't accustomed to what seemed like an enormous control room. Earth was in a new dimension of both time and space compared to his experience of reality traveling across the cosmos. He was amazed at how far six hundred feet was in terms of standard Earth distance. In the travel pod, he had once traveled nearly a light year in less time than he now needed to walk across the control room. Paradoxically, the control room now seemed very big compared to the solar systems he had traversed.

He kept himself occupied downloading volumes of data onto the control room computers. The systems were compatible with the modified pod, but the control room was a technological dinosaur by comparison. Of course, he took the precaution to build access codes into his files to prevent others from discovering their existence or content.

Meanwhile, Dr. Summers invested her time trying to debrief the aged Dr. Brenda Randal Davis. Her story was the only crucial link to what happened in the original near future that had set into motion the present events. Dr. Summers was an expert at interviewing people and getting into their thoughts, but this time it was not an easy task. An obvious role reversal had taken place. Her one-time understudy had become her superior in every way.

It was Brenda who spoke first. "My dear friend, I see so many questions in your eyes." Dr. Summers was not used to being read like a book. "But let's start with the obvious one— what happened in the original future." Dr. Summers was amazed at how Brenda was taking the lead so casually. She continued. "In the original future, you died before Nick and I got married. Four weeks after our wedding, Nick and I made the joint decision to test the travel pod. We imposed a seventy-two hour Code 1 Lockdown. Nick manned the control room while I entered the travel pod. I had no idea that I was pregnant, nor did we realize the travel pod would launch backward instead of forward in time." She stopped to control her tears. "Our goal was to compress time so I could complete my research to save Nick's mother. At our wedding, we learned that she was, or should I now say is, suffering from a terminal condition. After your death, we could not bear to lose her too."

Dr. Summers listened intently. Brenda continued, "The blast generated for the launch was much more severe than we had calculated. I have no way of knowing if Nick or the research facility survived it. Ironically, I survived by going backward instead of forward in time. At first, I contributed my nausea and constant sickness to trauma imposed by a new space and time dimension. It was three months before I realized I was pregnant. Paul was born one week shy of nine months into my journey." She paused to laugh. "I had no choice but to home educate." Dr. Summers joined the laughter. She well knew Brenda's aversion to home education.

Brenda continued. "It was actually Paul who figured out we were going backward instead of forward in time. I devoted my time and energy to my research while he mastered the other areas of knowledge on the computer banks. I may be biased, but I think we produced a genius."

Dr. Summers' mind was now moving into overload. Brenda continued. "This may sound strange, but it was not us who saved your life; it was actually you who saved our lives. Had you not responded to those hasty electronic messages and intercepted us exactly when you did, the travel pod would have been nothing more than a fancy casket going backward into endless time and space." She stopped to let that sink in. "It was also Paul who conceived of the plan for this intercept. It's amazing that it worked. We had years to plan, but you only had weeks."

"So where do we go from here?" asked Dr. Summers.

Brenda replied, "To quote an old mentor of mine, 'Containment is our greatest prudence.' It will be up to you to invest your new lease on life with caution and prudence. God has a design for life and death. Believe it or not, aging and death are a constant and necessary principle throughout the cosmos. Even stars and galaxies grow old and die." She then held up her old worn Bible. "For those who know God, death is just a new beginning. There is no eternal life apart from faith in Jesus Christ who is both the Creator and the Savior." There was no question that Dr. Brenda Randal Davis had become both an accomplished scientist and theologian. This was definitely a new side of Brenda that Dr. Summers had not previously known. One thing was for sure—the aged Dr. Randal Davis was now the one who commanded respect.

"Brenda, I need to ask you another question for very personal reasons." Dr. Summers paused. "Why did you so willingly treat me for my medical conditions but never undergo any regeneration treatment yourself?"

"I knew that question was coming." Brenda looked deep into Dr. Summers' eyes and said, "Most of my life has been spent trying to prevent death. The truth is that I always had a fear of death and dying. I wanted to find a way to avoid the inevitable and spare others from the same. I now know conclusively that we can prolong life, but we cannot prevent death. The greatest regeneration in life is not from sickness to health but rather from the physical realm into the spiritual and eternal realm. Even your new organic matter in your organs has the genetic age of your present life. The Creator has put a genetic clock in all cells that cannot be changed. Your illness has been cured, but your genetic clock has not been changed. You will not live longer than your original potential life span. I did not understand the reason for this until I read it in the Bible: 'It is appointed unto man once to die, then comes the judgment' (Hebrews 9:27). I have concluded that spiritual laws are higher than physical laws."

Dr. Randal Davis suddenly became quiet and closed her eyes in pain. She then drove home her final point. "Dr. Summers, you are a good scientist and humanitarian. I have learned much from you, and I know that you're very close to the truth about God. For a long time, I was too proud to concede the existence of God. Now my greatest anticipation is to meet Him face to face."

Brenda then reached out and grasped Dr. Summers' hand. "My body clock is not adjusting to the trauma of this dimensional time change. We anticipated this occurrence in my case. Both Paul and I are prepared for what is about to happen. In the pod is a very special place that Paul designed just for me. This pod must be launched again before the current Code 1 Lockdown comes to an end. Paul is working to prepare for the launch. The future is not yet written. By God's grace, you need to help write it well."

By this point, Paul was also by her side. She looked at both of them and smiled. Her final words were, "May God give the four of you wisdom and grace in your prudence." She then took a deep breath and closed her eyes for the last time. Both Paul and Julie sobbed.

Fifteen minutes before Code 1 Lockdown came to an end, there was a small tremor and a flash of light. Neither was detectable apart from very sensitive equipment. The highly improved antigravity launching mechanism had gone off without a hitch. Dr. Summers was relieved that the original nuclear launch system was no longer needed.

For the next forty-five minutes, Dr. Summers and the newly named Dr. Paul Randavis watched the scene from the control room. The full wall monitor recorded everything being transmitted from the pod as it streaked into its new orbit. Seeing it in high definition wasn't the same as being there in reality, but ten times light speed felt normal to Paul. It was like going home.

Not so for Dr. Summers. She nearly dug her fingernails through the upholstery of her chair trying to hang on. Three-dimensional cinemas have a very real effect on the bodily senses. The flight bag was a good idea. She couldn't control her motion sickness even though she hadn't actually moved.

Exactly forty-five minutes after launch, the screen went blank. This time it would be five weeks before additional data could be downloaded. The new programmed orbit would take the unmanned pod many times deeper into the cosmos than Paul had ever traveled. It had the potential of unlocking volumes of new data.

After staring into the blank screen for a few minutes, Dr. Summers turned to Paul and said, "Thank you for showing me your world." He had tears of loneliness and fear in his eyes. She then held his hand and said, "Now it's time for me to show you my world. I hope you're ready to meet your parents." She sighed. "If I have everything figured right, they will be about eighteen years younger than you. Of course for a while, you, the president, and myself are the only ones who will know your true identity. 'Dr. Randavis,' please wear this identification badge at all times. You obviously have the facility memorized, and your false identity information has already been entered into the system. Do you have any questions?"

"Just one," replied Dr. Randavis. "Would you pick me up for a dinner date? Keep in mind, I've never had real Earth food. I may also need a little private coaching in social graces. Just for the record, this is my first date—ever—so take it easy on me." He did not know it, but it would also be hers. As Dr. Summers looked into his eyes, fireworks exploded in her heart. He continued, "I'm also intrigued by the English word *romance*. Does it just happen between two people, or do you have to create it?"

For the next two minutes, the two experienced their very first romantic kiss. "Wow!" said Paul, "that was a ten times light speed rush!"

Dr. Summers blushed and smiled.

12

Restored Order

A short siren announced the end of Code 1 Lockdown. Immediately all doors opened, and the facility was cleared for normal operations. Faculty scurried to their various departments to begin initial assessments.

Nick and Brenda also went separate ways. Nick went to his former department and was relieved that everything checked out well. A few things had fallen to the floor and several windows were broken; apart from that, everything was secure. Brenda found basically the same but had a little trouble accessing all of her computer files. There was definitely a minor glitch in the system. Brenda was not an expert on computers, so she just noted the problem for the computer lab to check.

Every lab had some damage, though not major. It looked like they had been at the epicenter of an earthquake, but the construction of the facility had minimized the damage. If this had occurred in a civilian center, the damage would have been catastrophic.

At 3:00 p.m. the meeting commenced in the briefing room as planned. Dr. Davis opened the meeting, giving each department five minutes to present initial assessments. Every department reported some damage, but those located closest to the control room were damaged more severely. In fact, the engineering shop located next to the control room reported damages of a magnitude that would take nearly two months to repair.

Fortunately, there was no indication of radiation, confirming that the automatic entombing process had not been triggered. However, the projected damage to the control room did not look good. Nick reminded them that the control room itself was designed to absorb minor nuclear blasts expected with launches of a travel pod.

Nevertheless, two-thirds of the faculty urged Dr. Davis to launch Operation Blue Code as a precautionary measure. The staff geologist confirmed that whatever happened three days earlier had nothing to do with an ordinary earthquake. His equipment confirmed that it came from absorbing an impact from outer space rather than something from within the Earth's crust.

A few of the scientists became loud and animated. One stood up and demanded, "I call for a vote. I think Dr. Davis and Dr. Randal have lost their objectivity. I say we relieve them of their command and start Operation Blue Code immediately."

Brenda recognized him from earlier meetings with the secret society. It was obvious that he was the ring new leader, and as head of the computer lab, he had the ability to start Operation Blue Code without authorization. The situation was definitely out of control. Fear often has more influence over the human will than logic or reason. Unfortunately, even very educated people are not exempt from impulsive decision making when prompted by the demon of fear.

Just then, the security door at the front of the briefing room opened—a door that had only been used previously by Dr. Summers. A man and woman entered and proceeded to the lectern. When the woman turned, everyone gasped. "Okay, I want this meeting to come to order immediately," Dr. Summers snapped. "Let me remind you that you are all professional scientists, and I demand nothing short of professionalism." She stared at the scientist who was still standing after having demanded a vote. "Dr. Tompkins," she said, "as of this moment you are on probation. If I hear so much as a whisper against you in this facility in the next three years, you will be reassigned. Do I make myself clear?"

"Yes, Dr. Summers," he replied and sat down.

The voice and authority was definitely Dr. Summers', but the face and body looked twenty years younger.

One man quipped, "I don't know what hit that control room, but I wish my wife had been in there." It was the right touch of humor to change the atmosphere of the meeting. Even Dr. Summers managed a brief grin and slight blush.

Dr. Summers continued. "I am sure many of you have questions about what happened to me personally and to the research facility in general over the past three days of Code 1 Lockdown. Let me introduce my colleague, Dr. Randavis." There was brief applause. "He is my counterpart at a sister research facility. Over the past three days, we have participated in a joint top-secret test with his facility. A portion of this test included voluntary genetic regeneration, for which I volunteered due to my terminal medical condition." Dr. Summers paused to look in Brenda's direction. "Dr. Randal, you will be pleased to know that your research played a crucial role in the results standing before you at this moment. Let me just say that your selfless research helped to save my life."

Dr. Randal stood as the whole room erupted in applause.

Dr. Randavis then spoke. "Dr. Randal, I have personally and meticulously followed your research for many years." She was so young and beautiful just like he remembered from his childhood. He pushed back tears. "I performed the procedure myself, but believe me, you were standing over my shoulders." Again there was applause.

Dr. Randavis then looked at his father, Dr. Nick Davis, for the very first time in his life. Oh how he had longed to meet him and to just spend some father-son time. He had seen pictures, studied his writings, and even improved on his theories. Dr. Randavis could speak many languages, but at this moment he could not find words. Tears ran down his cheeks.

Dr. Summers wisely stepped in front of Dr. Randavis and took over the meeting. First impressions were not very positive. To many of the scientists, he seemed a little emotional for his position. She saved the moment by saying, "Tears of success are sweeter than tears of failure. You all played a vital role in this success." Many scientists had to wipe moist eyes when the impact of her words hit home. "Thank you all for your work and sacrifice."

She then looked at the clock and said, "I think you all have clean-up work to do. We will meet again in a few days to start debriefing. Dr. Randavis will lead many of these sessions." She paused. "You are all dismissed with the exception of Dr. Davis and Dr. Randal."

As the room emptied, Dr. Randal suppressed her emotions. She was obviously pleased to be accredited with the success of the experiment but felt slighted by this stranger. *Why wasn't I included in the medical procedure?* she wondered. *Who is this guy, and what part of my research did he steal to get these results?* She had known that her research had the potential for these results but believed they were at least two decades away from being able to produce anything like what was standing before her.

Once everyone else was gone, Dr. Summers spoke. "Dr. Davis and Dr. Randal, I want you to meet the newest member of our team. From now on, even I am subordinate to Dr. Randavis in terms of research direction and approval. Absolutely nothing will happen in this facility without his approval. Do I make myself clear?"

They both nodded. What a surprise! They knew if Dr. Summers was giving that kind of endorsement, whoever the guy was, he had to be very impressive.

Dr. Summers continued. "The two of you are about to learn some information that is so classified, that not even the president knows the full details." She turned to Dr. Randavis and said, "Open your mouth please." Dr. Summers took a cotton swab and collected a saliva sample. She put it in a sealed container and handed it to Dr. Randal.

Dr. Summers instructed, "Dr. Randal, you are the leading geneticist in the world. I want you to take this sample to my private lab and do a genetic analysis. Compare the results with our international DNA database. I want conclusive identification of both mother and father." She then turned to Dr. Davis. "Nick, you will accompany Dr. Randal through this entire procedure. When the computer prints the results, you will personally place them in a sealed envelope without either of you reading the document. At 8:00 p.m. this evening, the four of us will meet in the private executive dining hall. Please dress in semi-formal clothes and bring the sealed results with you." She looked at both of them and said, "You are dismissed."

13

SHOCKING DISCLOSURE

A Secret Service agent guided Dr. Randavis to his new quarters. As was her usual custom, Dr. Summers had missed no details. His room was equipped with a new wardrobe and refreshments. It was luxurious by any standard. The scene would have humored anyone watching in secret. His first taste of fountain cola did not go well; he emptied it down the drain and opted for water. Even the water had a strange taste compared to that of the travel pod.

The bed was wonderful, but it was gigantic. It was only queen-sized, but compared to his sleeping mat in the travel pod, it really was enormous. He was accustomed to a sleeping space about half the size of a twin bed. The bathroom was huge too. The travel pod had had a compact bathroom similar to one on a commercial airplane. Culture shock was beginning to hit hard. He missed his familiar surroundings, but they were long gone.

The Secret Service agent had orders to take him for a walk outside. Up to this point, he had only traveled in hallways inside the research facility. Dr. Summers had forgotten that during his entire life he had never ventured beyond the travel pod, control room, or the few hallways and underground rooms at the research facility. He had seen pictures of mountains, trees, and rivers but had no firsthand experience of what we thoughtlessly call nature.

The agent walked by his side in casual conversation, but when they stepped through a door into the outside recreation area, Dr. Randavis froze in his tracks. The sun was so brilliant and warm. The usual stars of the cosmos were no longer in sight. He was stunned by all of the new sights, sounds, and smells. He saw trees, birds, mountains, and clouds for the first time. Everything was so vast, so spacious. His sense receptors were going wild. He started speaking in a combination of German and Russian. The Secret Service agent quickly alerted security, and they in turn notified Dr. Summers.

A crowd quickly gathered around Dr. Randavis. He was in a daze. Eccentric people were common at the research facility, but he was on the edge—losing control. Just then, Dr. Summers burst through the door. Security was preparing to apprehend and immobilize him. A medical team led by a facility psychiatrist was about to give him a tranquilizer to calm him down until Dr. Summers ordered them all to stand down.

She ordered security to clear the plaza. Most of the people retreated to the dining area to watch the real-time screens. No one understood the meaning of what they were watching. No one knew that Dr. Randavis was experiencing planet Earth for the very first time. What they took for granted was more magnificent to him than the rest of the galaxy put together.

The two of them stood alone for several minutes while he collected himself. Tears streamed down his cheeks. She gently reached out and took his hand. She looked into his eyes and said, "Paul, I'm so sorry. I hadn't considered the shock this would be to you. Please forgive me."

He clung to her hand, almost squeezing the blood out of it. He whispered, "Nothing could have prepared me for this moment. This is so amazing! People who live here have no idea what a valuable treasure God has given them!" It was a good thing the conversation was not picked up by the cameras. It would have been very difficult to explain.

The two walked hand in hand very slowly. They stopped to feel the grass, to throw a ball, and even to examine things as common as an ant and a grasshopper. She touched a feather to his nose, and he sneezed. They both laughed. It was one thing to read about Earth; it was something altogether different and wonderful to experience it.

The flower garden was a special attraction. Dr. Randavis and Dr. Summers took a long time to smell every flower. For the first time in years, even Dr. Summers took time to smell the roses and to appreciate their beauty.

As the sun began to set over the mountains, the two stood alone hand in hand. "What a wonderful, strange, and different perspective of reality this presents," Dr. Randavis whispered quietly. He was now calm and totally in control again. "I feel like I have lived my life in a telescope experiencing the cosmos. It is beautiful but lifeless. Now I have stepped into a bioscope, and for the first time I can interact with other life. I have now seen the biggest and the smallest of God's creation. My mother was right. Everything He created proclaims His order, design, beauty, and power."

Dr. Summers spoke. "I don't know how to say this, but you are helping me to experience my own world for the very first time as well. I have studied it but neglected to experience it. I have taken so much for granted. The past seventy-two hours have changed my life. You have not preached to me, but you have helped me see the fingerprints of God. How can I thank you?"

"Well, there is one thing," he replied. "Would you please hold my hand through the next few months until I get totally adjusted to this place?"

She looked into his eyes and asked, "Is that an order or a request?"

He paused and said, "I think it's a mutual need. God did not create a man or a woman to be alone."

At 8:00 p.m., the four met in the executive dining room as planned. As the meal progressed, both Nick and Brenda wondered sarcastically what planet Dr. Randavis had come from. He sampled food like he was in a new culture. Some foods he liked, but others produced definite signs of aversion. It was almost comical watching him and Dr. Summers interact.

Finally, Dr. Randal could contain herself no longer. She had to ask the inevitable questions. "So, Dr. Randavis, what kind of school did you attend while you were growing up?"

He responded, "I guess you could say I was homeschooled by my mother." That touched a nerve with Brenda. She had repeatedly told Nick that homeschooling was out of the question for them. She viewed it as nothing but a wasted life for a woman.

Brenda continued her interrogation. "Okay, so where did you go to college?"

Without hesitation he said, "I was completely educated in my home. Much of it was through my mother until I exhausted her field of knowledge, then she turned me over to the computers and personal research."

By this point, a rude and sarcastic side of Dr. Randal was emerging. "Well," she retorted, "that explains your poor social skills. You are living proof that homeschooled children lack proper socialization. It must not have taken you long to empty your mother's brain."

Dr. Randavis replied, "My mother was very helpful in the beginning, especially in the areas of general science, genetics, and math. Much of my personal research started around age nine. I was on my own with history, astronomy, physics, engineering, linguistics, and foreign languages. She tried, but English, French, and Latin were all the languages she personally knew."

Brenda was becoming angry with this stranger. She not only felt that he was talking down to her, but he was also peeling her back like an onion. She was proud that she had personally mastered French and Latin beyond her English. She wasn't about to be put in her place by a sarcastic new superior who had obviously read her personnel file and was using it to jab her ego.

Dr. Summers interrupted her. "Did you have time to complete the genetic tests?"

Brenda knew she was being reeled in by the question. She responded, "Yes I did, and the results came back a lot faster than I anticipated."

Dr. Summers continued, "Have either of you seen the results?"

Nick replied, "No, we followed your directions to the letter. I did read the follow-up report that there was a 100 percent positive identification of both parents."

Dr. Summers smiled with approval. "Okay, Brenda," said Dr. Summers, "are you ready to learn the identity of our mystery guest? You're the expert, and you personally conducted the tests. I think you should be the one to read the results."

She grabbed the sealed envelope out of Nick's hand and said, "This should be good. Let's see what kind of socially dysfunctional gene pool you have bubbling in your veins." She started reading and then stopped in mid-sentence. "This can't be right. It's impossible!" She looked at Dr. Summers in shock and dropped the paper on the table. She then stared into the eyes of Dr. Randavis. She was starting to look just like Paul had looked after the first few minutes of stepping onto the plaza.

Nick picked up the paper and read: "With 100 percent accuracy, the mother is identified as Dr. Brenda Randal." He continued, "And with 100 percent accuracy, the father is identified as Dr. Nick Davis." He too was stunned into absolute silence.

Brenda stated, "So your name is short for Dr. Randal Davis?"

Dr. Summers and Dr. Randavis just nodded in agreement while trying unsuccessfully to hold back a few chuckles mixed with tears.

Dr. Summers spoke. "This is now about containment. Do you understand?" They both nodded. "I think it's time to catch the two of you up on the strange events of the past four weeks. A little over a month ago I received the following electronic message." She handed the transcript to them.

> *Dr. Summers, this is Paul again. Since our last correspondence, Mother died of old age. I calculated her age at ninety-five Earth years when she died. I calculate my own age now at close to 69.3 years of orbit time, ten weeks SET. I went over her calculations and discovered the problem. Our orbit sent us on a transverse time orbit to Earth. In other words, we have been traveling backward in time exactly twelve years for every fourteen days of Earth time . . . most of . . . equipment . . . still functional. I . . . think . . . cannot survive . . . orbit alone. . . . theoretically have . . . food . . . My loneliness . . . I occupy . . . time . . . only hope . . . you follow . . . detailed instructions . . . last message . . .*

After Nick and Brenda read the electronic message they sat in silence. Even Paul was surprised, because at his current age he had not yet written that message. Dr. Summers continued. "At first, I passed it off as a hoax, but then I started to do the math. Everything added up perfectly, and the theory matched what Dr. Davis had been proposing for time manipulation. Even though my condition was deteriorating fast, I purposed to see this thing through. I also calculated that another message would arrive in exactly fourteen days if there was any merit to the first message."

She continued. "Fourteen days later, to the second, I received a second message."

> *Dr. Summers, this is Paul again. Mother is now eighty-eight years old and very feeble. I do not think she has much time to*

live. I am now 57.3 years old. I am sure she will not survive the next orbit. She successfully completed the liver treatment and trained me on details of the surgery. You must prepare pod tunnel #2 to catch us for landing on June 13 at 3:00 p.m. Will be ready for emergency surgery. Do not go in for scheduled treatment . . . instead be in pod room . . . only hope . . . please be . . . Paul Davis . . . God bless!

Dr. Davis responded, "So that's why you issued the emergency work order to prepare tunnel #2 for a landing. This is absolutely amazing. Everything is starting to make sense."

"That's right," she said, "but there's much more to the story. In the original future, before the two of you got married, I died. At your wedding, you discovered that Nick's mother was terminally ill."

Dr. Davis looked surprised. "You mean my mother is sick?"

Dr. Summers continued, "Let me remind you that this is about containment. One month after your wedding, the two of you decided to test the travel pod. You declared a Code 1 Lockdown. Brenda, you entered the pod while Nick operated the control station. The explosion to launch the pod may have been disastrous. It was way beyond calculations. It is very possible that it destroyed at least the research facility if not far more. Fortunately, the pod was sent back in time instead of forward. Neither of you knew at the time, but Brenda was pregnant when she entered the pod."

Dr. Randavis continued. "I was born just under nine months into the flight. My home education was not by choice. Up until a few days ago, I lived my whole life inside the travel pod. I had the greatest teacher in the universe, and my classroom was a traveling science lab." He paused. "I don't know if I missed out or was blessed with a rare opportunity." He looked at the very young Dr. Randal. "Please forgive me, but the mother I

93

grew to know and love was older and more mature than you. It is hard for me to consider you my mother."

She blushed and nodded understandably.

He then turned to Dr. Davis. "By age twelve, I had already studied and researched all of your writings and works. I even compared them with great scientific minds from around the world. The exhaustive computer lab you placed in the travel pod was the key. It became my text for study. I admired you but never thought I would have the opportunity to meet you." He stopped to wipe tears from his eyes. By this time, they were all wiping away tears.

Paul continued, "Mother devoted herself to research. By the end of the first orbit she had much of her work completed. It was theoretical but very promising. I was approximately twelve years old. As we approached Earth, we prepared the pod for landing. Mother was excited about placing me in a university both to teach and to learn. You can imagine our shock when the pod went into automatic bypass, and we were instead flung back into space for a second orbit.

"For the first year, Mother slipped into depression. Her salvation came when she turned to a little black book. She started reading the Bible for several hours every day. She never did become religious, but she became godly."

Paul paused to look at Brenda. "I can't describe the transformation that followed. It was like she was seeing the universe and her research through new lenses. She became cheerful and found renewed joy in everything. Over the next five years, she made astounding breakthroughs not only in genetics but also in advanced medical procedures. By this time, we were working side by side as colleagues, with the exception that I also devoted myself to physics, astronomy, and engineering."

He closed his eyes and continued to talk. "We were forced to make many radical improvements to the travel pod. During the second orbit, our goal also changed. Instead of trying to return to Earth for a landing, we decided to devote ourselves to the discovery of new laws of physics and modification of archaic theories. Our primary guiding principle was that we both had to agree 100 percent before any new theories were tested or improvements made. Mother was a stickler for detail, and that saved our lives several times. Unfortunately, the second orbit also ended with the pod switching into automatic bypass. This was disappointing but not disabling."

He continued. "With the modifications finished on the travel pod, we anticipated new capabilities and experiments. I made significant improvements on the antigravity propulsion mechanism. The basic design theory was on track, but it had to be interfaced with the nuclear reactor for smoother acceleration and control. The on-board engineering department was great but very thin on raw material. It demanded much more power than the original designers had anticipated. It performed well at slow speeds, under two times the speed of light; beyond that it was sluggish and even hazardous."

Dr. Davis raised his eyebrow at that statement. "You mean it is possible to break the light barrier?"

Dr. Randavis continued. "Oh yes, it is possible to do that and much more." He then continued with his story. "With the new modifications we were able to change our orbit and explore significantly the depths of space. The only catch was, we needed to maintain our axis contact with Earth on time in the event that a landing was possible. Future travel pods can easily be modified to alleviate the need for the tunnels and orbits altogether, but we did not have enough raw material for the refit." He paused. "We did find a way to collect heavy metal particles and even gases while traveling through galactic nebula, but we didn't have the technical equipment to utilize them for development."

By this point, Dr. Davis was ecstatic, and his imagination ran wild. He was full of questions and couldn't wait to see the travel pod and the modifications.

Dr. Summers intervened and encouraged Dr. Randavis to continue. "It was during our third orbit that we discovered and crossed our first radical time and space warp. By radical I mean it wrapped around so tightly that the edges began to run parallel with each other. It wasn't the normal curvature that you postulated in your original theory. By cutting directly through the warp at 90 degrees, we were able to reach relative speeds that exceeded 25x to 50x light year. It was hard to calculate our actual speed, but in several months of travel, we were literally propelled thousands of light years across the universe."

Dr. Randal was beginning to wonder if the conversation had moved into science fiction. Besides, she was much more interested in the genetic and medical benefits of the experiments.

By this point, Dr. Randavis' three dinner companions were on the edge of their seats. His story was so amazing that they didn't even bother to eat. He continued. "It was toward the end of the third orbit that a strange thought occurred to me. The time travel theory was sound but never tested. I asked Mother, 'Could it be possible that we were launched backward in time instead of forward?' That might explain why we had not been received for landing. It also implied that we would forever be in automatic bypass from Earth. With the window of opportunity quickly closing, I prepared my first electronic message. This may sound strange, but I do not recognize the two messages that Dr. Summers just presented. I obviously sent them when I was older than I am now. Opposite time and space continuums are constantly intersecting. Reality going backward is constantly meeting the reality moving forward. The amazing thing is that we had no perceptual indication that we were the ones moving backward in time. All the physics in our dimension were functioning properly."

Dr. Summers interrupted. "This is why containment is so important with this experiment. We have unleashed something much more dangerous and unpredictable than a collision of nuclear particles. We are talking about a collision of space and time realities. We have effectively added new matter to the universe by duplicating travel pod #1 at least twice. We now have three Dr. Randals, two of which have already died of old age. We also have two mature Dr. Randavises, the original of whom has not even been conceived yet. We have Paul sitting with us at this table and most likely an older one who sent these two messages floating somewhere in the distant past."

Dr. Randal interjected, "We also have a very healthy and reproductively restored scientist who should have already died. Don't get me wrong, Dr. Summers, but you now have the potential of marrying, bearing children, and dying of old age. It just dawned on me that my research has already altered the future." She then added with a chuckle, "It doesn't look to me like you will be dying anytime soon, and it seems like you've taken quite a liking to our son. The whole facility is buzzing with talk of your new romantic flame."

Dr. Summers turned red and asked, "What are you talking about?"

Brenda laughed. "The cameras were on when you and Paul cleared the plaza for your first date."

Nick joined the laughter and added, "Romance and physics do have a lot in common, and they are both full of mysteries."

14

REASONABLE CONTAINMENT

The meeting ended, as usual, with more questions than answers. That's often the case whenever scientists review the results of experiments that didn't go exactly as planned. Nick and Brenda were extremely disappointed when they learned that the modified pod had been launched back into orbit. However, they supported the decision, understanding the need for containment. They were relieved to learn that Dr. Randavis had downloaded all of the pod's research data onto Dr. Summer's private computer terminal. It was not integrated with the rest of the system, so it was considered to be contained and very safe.

Responsibility for Dr. Randavis' socialization would be divided equally among the other three. Nick and Paul became roommates for a little over a month. This arrangement went a long way in helping Paul to learn domestic skills. The two became close friends but never did step into a father-son kind of relationship. It was just too awkward for both of them with Paul being over fifteen years Nick's senior. However, as professional colleagues, they became an amazing team. Paul was impressed with Nick's aptitude and love for physics and astronomy. It was a refreshing change after having spent his entire life with a devoted geneticist. Dr. Davis was a very good student and a fast learner. His imagination quickly bridged the gap between theory and his personal lack of intergalactic travel. Of course, Paul's detailed research notes were of great help. Nick pored over them like a child in a candy shop. Brenda and Julie actually became a bit jealous of the tight bond the two men shared.

The wedding plans went forward according to schedule but with a few minor twists. While they were careful not to tamper too much with the original future, a few weeks before the wedding, Dr. Randal and Dr. Randavis arranged to perform surgery on Nick's mother—something Nick told her was "routine preventative surgery."

Recent blood tests were not normal and had pointed to potential problems. Her trusted family doctor had strong hunches concerning her condition and had insisted that she see the regional specialist immediately.

She had every intention of doing just that until she received a very timely and persuasive call from her eldest son. Nick had somehow accessed her medical information and turned it over to what he called "the best doctors in the universe." He ensured his mother that they could correct the problem with a very minor and nonintrusive procedure, and she opted to follow her son's wise counsel.

A special surgical room was prepared in a VA hospital in California. The entire wing was off-limits to regular hospital staff for one week. Hospital administration was simply told that "experimental equipment" would be moved in for the procedure and then promptly removed. That usually meant "top-secret" and was not questioned. The hospital staff assumed the identity of the patient, and not the so-called experimental equipment, was the real secret. They speculated about which world leader was sharing their facility. It had happened numerous times before, though the new equipment was an unusual twist.

Meeting a future daughter-in-law for the first time is always unnerving, but meeting her while wearing a surgical gown and lying on her operating table was really awkward. Brenda seemed a bit old to Mrs. Davis to become her daughter-in-law, but at the same time, way too young to be her surgeon. The two roles were a good balance.

Nick's mother was relieved to meet the older and more seasoned staff surgeon who was supervising the procedure. He seemed to add credibility to the whole medical process. It's a good thing she did not know he was actually her unborn first grandson.

Dr. Randal performed the procedure as Dr. Randavis observed. She was extremely skilled. During the procedure, they observed a few additional areas in need of a little touch-up work. The temptation was simply too great to resist. After ten children, she needed a few things tightened up. By the wedding day, she felt great and looked remarkable. Friends said she looked more like the bride than the mother of the groom!

Because of their mutual government security clearance and association with the current administration, Nick and Brenda's fathers had become good friends. Nevertheless, it was still a little strange having them together for the wedding. Reverend Davis performed the ceremony, and Nick's nine siblings were all in the wedding. It was a bit chaotic but fun. Ironically, Paul enjoyed them the most. In many ways he had missed out on his childhood and had a lot of catching up to do. It was hard for him to imagine that these children were actually his aunts and uncles!

The building was nearly full and surrounded by security. When the traditional wedding march began, Mrs. Davis stood up and turned around. Following her lead, the entire congregation, including the president of the United States and the First Lady, also stood. One by one, five bridesmaids made their way to the platform. They were much more comfortable in lab gowns than bridesmaid dresses, but they all looked beautiful. Finally, with the entire wedding party in place, Mr. Randal appeared at the back of the church with a beautiful bride on each arm. They walked together down the long aisle. The two smiling brides joined Paul and Nick at the front of the church. Nick and Brenda exchanged vows first, then Paul and Julie.

A few guests commented on the similarity of their names—Randal, Davis, Randavis—but no one gave it a second thought. To avoid confusion, Paul decided to take on Dr. Summers' last name, so at the end of the service, Reverend Davis concluded by announcing, "Ladies and gentlemen and distinguished guests, I present to you Mr. and Mrs. Randal Davis and Mr. and Mrs. Paul Summers." The crowd erupted in applause as the newlyweds made their exit.

At the reception, each man produced an elegantly wrapped gift for his bride. Neither man had told the other what he was giving. Brenda opened hers first. She was surprised to unwrap a shiny new Bible with gold engraving. It read: "Most Cherished of All Gifts on Our Wedding Day." Underneath, in smaller print, were the words: "From Your Loving and Faithful Husband, Nick Davis." She was deeply touched but had no idea of the future significance of the gift. She only knew it represented her husband's heart and soul.

Paul then handed a gift to his cherished new bride. He had never attended a wedding before, but he gave the only gift he knew would be appropriate. Julie opened her gift. As she looked down, her eyes focused on a very old and worn Bible. The writing had been refreshed with new gold engraving. It said: "Most Cherished of All Gifts on Our Wedding Day." Underneath, in smaller print, were the words: "From Your Loving and Faithful Husband, Paul Summers." She recognized the worn Bible and began to cry. The two embraced, more out of respect for a special guest who was not able to make the ceremony. How Julie had cherished her short time with the aged Dr. Randal Davis! She knew the gift represented Paul's most precious memories from his years in the travel pod.

Reverend Davis was impressed. Years earlier he had given a similar gift to his young bride. It had been his prayer that this would be a tradition that would continue for generations to come. He was surprised that Dr. Summers had come from a family that practiced the same tradition.

The two couples honeymooned at a private executive retreat center in Hawaii reserved for top international dignitaries. The honeymoon lasted just over a week. Security was tight and a little awkward. Paul's three travel companions were amazed that he could communicate so fluently in the native language of the facility staff—all locals hired from the community—as their language was spoken only on a few obscure islands. He also communicated fluently in the language of fifteen other international dignitaries sharing the facility.

Within days, Paul had been recruited to serve as an informal translator by nearly everyone at the retreat center. And although his wife was impressed with his translating skills, she was also obviously annoyed by the distraction. Shortly, the Secret Service intervened and put a stop to the activity. Dr. Julie Summers saw to that little detail herself.

Paul adjusted well to the tropics. He especially enjoyed the waves splashing on his body as he sat for hours in knee-deep water on the beach. He and his wife held hands, went on long walks, and even tried scuba diving. Prior to the trip, his skin was pale from having never been exposed to the sun. Thanks to a lot of sunscreen and then suntan lotion, he eventually took on a pleasing tan. His wife did seem to mother him a bit, but he relished the attention. By this point, his daily exercise routines were paying off, and masculine, well-defined muscles were emerging. The couple became the talk of the retreat center. They looked and acted like thirty-year-old, successful yuppies rather than middle-aged scientists.

Though much younger, Nick and Brenda strained to keep up with their older counterparts. However, they were also having the time of their lives. The two couples had different interests, so by the third day, they spent much of their time apart. Nick and Brenda gravitated towards cultural events while Paul and Julie had fun simply experiencing their surroundings.

Both couples lamented when the time came to return to the familiar surroundings of the research facility. Paul had infused new life and energy into his three friends. They were discovering that it is possible to be respected intellectuals and to enjoy childlike adventure at the same time.

Upon their return to the research facility, they were met with a huge surprise celebration. The staff was becoming more like family than work associates. They pulled out all the stops for these festivities.

The biology department brought out genetically modified fruit with flavor so succulent that rare hummingbirds were drawn from miles away. The hummingbirds actually became a main attraction during the celebration.

The underwater fireworks display in the recreational swimming pool was absolutely beautiful. Streams of different colored liquid gushed into the air with flaming sparks emitting from them. Then the liquid evaporated into the air just before reaching the ground. Lingering in the air was the brilliant fragrance of fresh flower blossoms.

The florescent sound wave display was also amazing. With this technology, songs could be seen as well as heard. Each tone had a corresponding light signature. As the music played, sound waves were slowed just enough to enter the visible spectrum. Each note appeared to be dancing with the others across the plaza.

The night ended with a ride around the plaza in a floating carriage made of transparent aluminum and tinted with gold. Antigravity experiments had come a long way during the past month, thanks to some lectures and drawings by Paul Summers. The four honored guests were the first ones to test ride the new technology. With the controls of antigravity back in his hands, Paul couldn't resist a little showmanship. He pulled off several precision daredevil stunts like a professional stunt pilot. He seemed right at home, but his three companions turned green from motion sickness. The look on Julie's face told him it was time to land. The carriage came to a halt right in front of a red carpet leading into the decorated dining hall.

It was clear that the staff had worked hard to prepare for the homecoming of these two newlywed couples. The window monitors in the dining hall played video clips of the honored guests. They included highlights of when Nick and Brenda first met at the science fair years earlier. They looked so young. It brought laughs from everyone, including them. It was revealing to see how many times they had lingered around each other's exhibit prior to the firestorm that drove them so far apart.

Also captured on video was Paul and Julie Summers' first date—their walk across the plaza. She blushed at several scenes which appeared much more romantic on the screen than she recalled in real life. By this point, Paul was well liked by everyone, but still there was mystery surrounding him, and that was unsettling to several of the staff.

15

THE TRAP

Following a routine briefing with department heads, Dr. Paul Summers was asked what his views were concerning origins. It was not an innocent question as Dr. Tompkins had been contriving for weeks to ensnare Summers in some controversy. Origins was an inflammatory subject among scientists even at the research center and usually led to a no-win discussion that served only to inflame animosity and cement bias. Even though Tompkins' question had taken Dr. Summers quite by surprise, his response appeared to have been well rehearsed.*

Dr. Summers began in a most unexpected way. "Well, since the Bible contains the oldest reputable record of origin, let's start there. 'In the beginning,' Genesis 1:1. Every theory of origin recognizes a beginning, or an absolute starting point, for the physical matter in the universe. Both the first and second laws of thermodynamics point to an absolute starting point of all energy and matter. Albert Einstein's theory of relativity points

---

* The Bible urges Christians to "always be ready to give a defense to everyone who asks you a reason for the hope that is in you" (1 Peter 3:15). Dr. Paul Summers is ready; are you? Truth Quest bonus material is included at the back of this book to further equip you to answer skeptics such as Dr. Tompkins.

to an absolute beginning. When the expansion of the universe is reversed and pulled back to a central spot in space, the picture of a Big Bang is not difficult to imagine. The debate starts with the next two words: 'God created.'"

Dr. Tompkins let out a deep and disruptive sigh at the mention of God as if to communicate his disgust with the direction this was going, but others respectfully encouraged him to continue.

"The word *beginning* might better be translated 'head' rather than 'beginning.' At the head, God created the heavens and the earth. This would stress not the beginning of time but rather the beginning of events in the process of origin.

"Without a source of energy, there could be no beginning, no starting point. According to the biblical text, in the beginning God was all that existed. He is the Head, the One who caused all that followed to happen. Romans 1:20 in the New Testament says, 'For since the creation of the world His invisible attributes, His eternal power, and divine nature are clearly seen, being understood through what has been made, so they are without excuse.' The Genesis record then, the history of our origins, opens with the existence of an eternal, intelligent, all-powerful Being—God.

"And to create is the first activity attributed to God. In the Hebrew language it is the word *bara* and refers to the initiation of an object, not the manipulation of something already existing. Man with his technology can invent, but only God can create. The writer of the book of Hebrews describes the work of creation clearly. Hebrews 11:3 says, 'By faith we understand that the worlds were prepared by the word of God, so that what is seen was not made out of things that are visible.' God made everything from nothing."

At this point, Dr. Tompkins interrupted. "So where did God come from?" This derails most debates, but Dr. Summers didn't miss a beat.

"Thank you for that question! With his polite and respectful response, even Dr. Tompkins began to lend a listening ear.

"It has been said that God exists outside of the realm of time and space, but technically, the time that applies to God is eternity. God's name is Yahweh, or Jehovah, which means 'the Eternal, Self-Existent One.' He always was and always will be.

"Belief in the existence of God is an act of faith, but not blind faith. It is faith based on evidence. From the time God introduces Himself in Genesis 1:1, He begins to set forth evidence of His own existence. Embracing atheism, or the belief that there is no God, without examining the evidence He set forth in the Bible is a leap of blind faith into nonbelief.

"The concept of eternality is hard to comprehend because human experience only knows the temporary. Living organisms are born, and they die. Material things are made, and then they wear out. Experience teaches us that all things, including time, have a beginning and an end. You have asked, Dr. Tompkins, 'Where did God come from?' But questions of when and where relate to the natural realm of time and space. These questions force the supernatural into the box of natural understanding. Finite man will never comprehend the infinite God within the confines of human experience."

For the next two hours Dr. Summers dissected, verse-by-verse, the first two chapters of the book of Genesis, carefully and thoroughly examining how the principles of modern science confirm the Creation account in every aspect. His presentation was impressive and easy to follow. He didn't take shots at any particular position; he just laid out a very logical case. To the surprise of Dr. Tompkins, most of his colleagues were transfixed by Summers' arguments. Dr. Tompkins, however, countered angrily, "Your views are driven out of religious bias! This is not science; it's religion! You Christians are all alike! You refuse to open your minds to the evidence because you are prejudiced towards a God!"

Paul responded by saying, "Every scientist brings some form of prejudice into the laboratory. Atheism brings an anti-God prejudice into scientific theory and research. Intelligent Design advocates bring a different set of lenses into the lab. It's important to understand both models as the data must be equally tested and filtered through both. Time has a way of causing truth to come to the surface."

At this point, a tense restlessness overshadowed the conversation. There was a very defined polarization of opinions. This was the first time the intimidation of Dr. Tompkins had allowed open conversation on the subject, and the guiding principle of professional respect which had historically governed the research facility was now being strained. Dr. Julie Summers stepped in and brought the conversation to a close. Her suggestion was for the group to move into the cafeteria, hoping the informal atmosphere would produce a more casual conversation. Her hopes were short-lived.

16

PRIVATE INVESTIGATION

Dr. Tompkins wasted no time setting out to destroy Drs. Paul and Julie Summers. Believing he was acting totally under the radar of the four facility directors, he convinced the secret society to conduct an in-depth search into the background and true identity of Paul Summers. He was now more convinced than ever that he was an imposter. No university would ever give a quack like him a degree, let alone a doctorate in science. Dr. Tompkins could smell a rat, and he was determined to sniff him out.

The official government file on Dr. Summers did not check out in every detail. It looked more like a bogus profile put together for a witness protection program. There was no doubt that he was a genius; however, his country of origin and his educational background were sketchy. Some speculated that either he was there through an exchange program with another country, or he had been given secret asylum by the government.

Many international scientists had been recruited to work at the research center, and it was usually easy to pin down their country of origin. Most of them spoke English as a second language, but Paul Summers could converse fluently in any language! Many times during briefings he would answer difficult and even technical questions in both English and the native tongue of the staff person asking the question. He was either a linguistically gifted genius or a biological humanoid computer.

One of the ophthalmologists in the secret society had developed a way to use a retina scanalizer within the security system to determine brain function. He noted that average people use less than 10 percent of their brain capacity. Those in the dietary and maintenance departments averaged 7 to 8 percent. Security and special agents at the facility came in at 14 percent. And the research scientists there consistently registered 16 to 18 percent, which is unusually high. He impressed everyone when he noted that prior to Code 1 Lockdown, a reading of Dr. Julie Summers' brain function showed that she was utilizing 21 percent of her active brain capacity. However, after her physical metamorphosis—or whatever it was that had turned her into a supermodel—her brain function had increased from 21 percent to an astounding 32.5 percent! Whatever had happened during that lockdown included much more than a surgical procedure.

One of the more cynical members of the secret society verbalized what everyone else was thinking. "I wonder if we're dealing with the same Dr. Julie Summers who was somehow made new and better or an entirely different Julie Summers."

The ophthalmologist's response did little to solve the mystery. "Everything else in her retina test is exactly the same. There's just not enough information for me to give you a conclusive answer. I'm quite certain, though, that you'll find this interesting. Dr. Paul Summers has used his retina identification test only one time to gain access to a room. Usually accompanied by others, he allows them to open security doors. Yesterday, though, he entered the briefing room alone, leaving his first retina image that my department can analyze. I need to double-check the equipment to ensure that it's functioning properly, but the scanalizer recorded an astounding 89 percent active brain function!" The entire group gasped.

"How can you explain this phenomenon?" asked one scientist.

The neurologist in the group provided an answer. "I'm in the process of conducting other neurological tests on Dr. Summers, by invitation of course. I can confirm that he is 100 percent human although exceptionally developed in brain capacity. Since brain function is determined by the stimulation received mostly during one's developmental years, and since he comes in at slightly below the national average in the area of socialization and relational skills, he most likely was deprived of contact with others during much of his early childhood.

"In all other areas of active brain function, he is developed way beyond any person ever documented. He undoubtedly experienced something so out of this world in his formative years that his brain demanded and imprinted full active function. We have known for years that this is possible; we just haven't discovered a stimulus strong enough or challenging enough to produce full brain activation." He paused. "I also surmise that the 11.5 percent jump in Dr. Julie Summers came from experiencing some kind of phenomenal stimuli that forced her to activate new brain function despite her age. I am more inclined to think in terms of these natural explanations than some kind of conspiracy. I have the utmost respect for both of them and am very thankful that they are leading our team."

The mechanical engineer interrupted. "This might also help to explain why the carriage with the antigravity propulsion unit responded so well with Dr. Summers at the controls during their 'welcome home' reception. We could barely get it to go up or down, forward or backward, but with him at the controls, it could do phenomenal stunts. It was as if it were an extension of his subconscious mind."

The neurologist spoke again. "In his case, the subconscious and the conscious functions of the brain are fully integrated. This explains why he can transition between languages so fluently without pausing to think. I personally believe he is much closer to the normal function and capacity for which man was originally created—"

Dr. Tompkins rudely cut him off. "Alright, let's stay away from religion; it has no place in science. I would rather point to evolved alien life forms or extra-terrestrials involved in the origin of life on Earth than to succumb to the notion of a God. From this point on, any reference to a supreme designer is prohibited in these meetings."

The neurologist politely challenged him. "Just because you lead this little society of ours doesn't mean I accept or honor your negative bias. As scientists, we boast of being open-minded, yet I find it paradoxical that our field has more intellectual censorship than any other discipline of learning. I would hardly let your 18 percent active brain capacity be my final guide to truth." He paused. "For that matter, I would not even allow Dr. Paul Summers, with 89 percent active brain capacity, dictate my views. He may be a genius, but he still knows only a fraction of 1 percent of all the knowledge in the universe. The Earth is very small compared to the universe. By comparison, planet Earth is far less than a grain of sand on a remote beach compared to the rest of the known cosmos. We have a very small and limited perspective from which to build our understanding of reality. Only a fool would draw conclusions based on such restricted data."

He then admonished the entire group. "We are professional scientists, and we must stop looking for a conspiracy behind everything. I know we have different guiding principles and values, but this tension is good because it ensures balance." He then looked at the group leader. "By assuming and looking for a conspiracy behind everything at this research facility, you have turned this noble society into a conspiracy itself. To be honest, I'm beginning to question your motives and the way you are manipulating the direction of this group."

The neurologist's point was well taken, and his arguments were sound. Censorship is an enemy of science no matter which side imposes biased restrictions. Philosophical bias and political agendas drive the interpretation of more so-called science than educators at any level are willing to admit.

Dr. Tompkins was not used to being challenged at society meetings. He had made the false assumption that they shared his vendetta against Dr. Paul Summers, or at least backed his liberal causes. The group was changing. Seasoned scientists usually go through a metamorphosis. They are seldom as gullible or controlled by bias as their new intern counterparts coming fresh out of universities. Most of the original secret society members had matured during their tenure at the research facility, and they were no longer willing to be controlled or to act as pawns for any special-interest group.

The leader backed down because he recognized that he was on thin ice—particularly since his recent rebuke and probation. He quickly changed the subject to get himself out of the spotlight, but he didn't comprehend the full measure of what the neurologist was saying. Tompkins' control was gone, his agenda had been exposed, his motives were clearly impure, and his influence was evaporating. Nevertheless, like a bloodhound on a hot trail, he continued. "We do have one recourse. If there is a way we can obtain a genetic sample from Dr. Paul Summers without his knowledge, we could then do a genetic analysis and look for abnormalities. I know the former Dr. Randal has been out of favor with this group for a while, but I now have a connection with one of her new subordinates in the genetics department, and I think I could ask him for a favor."

A fool might hide behind academic credentials, but he is still a fool. Dr. Tompkins was not motivated by a quest for truth but rather by an appetite for control and power. He was jealous of Dr. Julie Summers and her position as director over the research facility, and he worked tirelessly behind the scenes towards her demise. He would not be satisfied until he sat in her chair and displayed his name over her office. He lamented that he had come so close to pulling off Operation Blue Code. Had it succeeded, he was confident that he would have been voted in as the new director. Dr. Julie Summers would have been gone forever, and he would have been out from under her shadow. Pride and envy had a deep grip on him.

He was oblivious to the fact that her position and authority had come directly by appointment from the president of the United States and not by way of popular vote. Nor did he understand that she was serving her country in a capacity much larger than overseeing the research center. She also worked for the department of Homeland Security and the Central Intelligence Agency. The president had appointed her because of her academic credentials, character, long history of service to her country, and unquestionable integrity. She was there because of her loyalty and had no personal agenda. What a contrast!

17

THE PUBLIC TRAP

Most of the group had, at one time or another, seen and even fallen prey to Dr. Tompkins' intimidation and conversational traps. Everyone, including Tompkins, knew that he had come up on the short side of the informal debate a few weeks earlier in the conference room. He despised the fact that Paul Summers, although obviously biased towards Intelligent Design, hadn't come across as vicious or dogmatic. He had simply encouraged people to think and to weigh the evidence for themselves. Paul was gaining significant respect while promoting an intellectually open environment for discussion.

It wasn't long before Tompkins coerced Paul into another random discussion that he had hoped would lead to the subject of theology. As they neared the dining hall, Dr. Tompkins set his trap. It was his goal to make Dr. Summers come across as more of a preacher than a reputable scientist. He was certain that if he let him talk long enough, he would get to the heart of religion. At that point, Dr. Tompkins would bring the mock-and-ridicule hammer down with great force. It was his hope that many in the dining area would overhear the conversation without the context of the previous discussion in the conference room. His goal was to verbally crush and discredit the newcomer in the eyes of his colleagues.

As they rounded the corner, Dr. Tompkins simply asked, "How does the Mars Proposition fit into your worldview, and what does it say about the unique place of man in the universe?"

The bait was taken. Without skipping a beat, Dr. Summers launched into the subject. He picked up right where he'd left off two weeks earlier. "I'm glad you reminded me! Genesis 2 gives a more detailed account of Creation and the problem-solving process that God went through in starting, sustaining, and spreading life across planet Earth. Verse 5 simply says, 'Now no shrub of the field was yet in the earth, and no plant of the field had yet sprouted, for the Lord God had not sent rain upon the earth; and there was no man to cultivate the ground.'

"Think with me for a moment. What if one's objective was not to discover life on Mars but rather to start life on Mars. What would human technology and science need to do in order to successfully populate the red planet? We are still many decades away from having the technology needed to pull off this proposition, but considering it may shed light on the mystery of how life started on our own planet.

"Without a source of light there would be no chance of starting life on Mars. Fortunately, because the Sun in our solar system already provides light on the red planet, we wouldn't have to start from scratch. After light, the most important elements would be air and water. We'd need to build a dome and fill it with the right balance of oxygen and other gases, and we'd need to build a large reservoir and irrigation system. Not surprisingly, the above scenario is basically what Genesis records as God's first steps in preparing planet Earth to support life!

"Next, the challenge would be to introduce self-propagating life. At this point we would need to choose either the evolutionary model or the creation model to ensure that life takes root and begins to flourish. In other words, after all the time, energy, and technology invested in the project, do you think we would start with one simple cell and hope that other biological life forms eventually evolve from it, or would it be better to introduce many separate species of life as complete, fertile, and functioning species? Wouldn't we all choose to guide the process with the intelligent and selective guidance of the scientific community rather than rely on random chance?

"Now, assuming we'd introduce many species of life, is there a logical order in which to introduce them? Wouldn't we move progressively from plant life, through marine and insect life, and eventually to advanced mammals? Well, guess what? That is the exact order God used in the creation of life on Earth!

"So if the Genesis account is basically the way modern science would approach the Mars Proposition, why is it so difficult to accept it as a valid model or account of the origin of life on Earth? This hypothetical Mars Proposition proves the biblical model is not only feasible but also the model of choice. Why is there so much controversy? It all comes down to the origin, role, and purpose of mankind, which was the second part of your question.

"The words recorded in Genesis 1:26, 'Let Us make man in Our own image,' are important because they present the truth that man did not evolve into the highest life form; rather, God very purposefully created man as the crowning achievement of all His creative work.

"This has monumental implications for your life. You are neither a mutation nor a mistake. You have meaning, value, dignity, and purpose because God created you in His own likeness. You have been endowed with special gifts and abilities that no animal can match. As a human, you also have a calling on your life. This is where meaning, purpose, and direction in life come from. This calling is to enter into a personal relationship with God. God loves you and wants to reveal Himself to you. But there is a problem.

"God is good, just, and holy and will not allow sin into His presence. People have rejected God, taken His name in vain, worshiped everything and anything in place of God, displaced Him as the Creator with the theory of evolution, dishonored their parents, killed, became immoral in thought or deed, stolen, lied, and coveted things to fill the voids in their lives. These behaviors are sin, and they drive a wedge between people and God. Every person has sinned, and because of sin, fellowship with God is broken. Few of us have broken all of God's Commandments, but all of us have broken some. Just as it takes only one broken link for a whole chain to be broken, so it takes only one violation of the Ten Commandments for the whole law to be broken.

"This explains why so many people feel lost and separated from God with no meaning, purpose, or peace in life. The Bible teaches that we can become slaves of our own sinful ways, making life miserable for others and ourselves. This is where all the pain and suffering in the world comes from. The Bible teaches in Romans 6:23 that, 'the wages of sin is death.' We need to be saved not only from our sin but also from ourselves.

"Fortunately, the rest of the Bible has good news. The mighty God, Creator of the universe, provided a way to forgive man of his sins and to restore a loving relationship between Himself and sinful people. The solution was His Son, Jesus Christ, the only one to ever perfectly keep God's Law.

"Because Jesus was sinless, He did not have a death sentence on His life, yet He died on a cross. Why? You are about to learn the most important truth in the whole Bible. Jesus loves you so much that He gave *His* life to pay for *your* sins. He took *your* punishment and paid *your* wages of sin.

"After His death, Jesus was put in a grave. But because of who He is, death could not hold Him. After three days, Jesus rose from the dead!

"Jesus has done everything necessary for your sin barrier to be removed. He wants to forgive your sin, and He invites you into a wonderful relationship with Him, but He will not force Himself on anyone. In order to receive forgiveness of sin and the gift of eternal life, you must trust Him to be your personal Savior. It involves confessing to God that you're a sinner and being willing to repent or turn from your sinful ways. Becoming a Christian involves turning over control of your life to God. In simple but sincere faith, you can talk to Jesus and ask Him to forgive your sins and become your Savior.

"You may consider using the following prayer as a guide: 'Dear Lord Jesus, I know I'm a sinner and that I need Your forgiveness. I believe that You died for my sins and that You paid my debt in full on the cross. I repent and confess my sins to You. Please forgive me and come into my heart and life as You said You would. I trust You as my Savior, and I will follow You as my Lord. Thank You for answering my prayer.'

"Becoming a Christian is like becoming a new creation. God begins a work of change in your heart and life. Remember those activities God the Creator did in the first two chapters of the Bible? The Holy Spirit will start doing some of those same kinds of things in your life. He will separate the light from the darkness and rearrange things to——."

"Okay, I've heard enough!" shouted Dr. Tompkins in utter disgust. "You've suddenly turned into a preacher rather than a scientist. I don't have time for this nonsense. I'm an intelligent, self-directed man. The only savior our world needs will be a brilliant scientist—someone like me who will discover or invent things to help our world become a utopia." Then he abruptly stood up and stormed out. He was confident that his theatrical exit would punctuate his mocking of Dr. Paul Summers.

18

SHOCKING DISCLOSURE

Dr. Tompkins had managed to get Dr. Paul Summers' genetic sample from a balloon he had blown up to use as an illustration during one of his briefings. The balloon had been delivered to Dr. Tompkins by one of his newest and most trusted recruits, and fortunately it contained enough saliva to conduct the test. Tompkins was confident that the results would reveal his true identity and finally solve the mystery surrounding Dr. Paul Summers.

Tompkins personally delivered the balloon to the genetics department and supervised the test. Within a few hours, the results were complete. Five people watched with glee via closed-circuit television as he read the results. The report read: "No genetic abnormalities." It was a major disappointment for Tompkins. But the next revelation was a real shocker: "100 percent positive identification. Father is Fred Randy. Occupation: Coal miner. Marital Status: Divorced. Mother is Martha Navis. Occupation: Café waitress. Marital Status: Single unwed mother."

Dr. Tompkins pulled out a pencil from his pocket and began to scribble on the top of the report. The hidden camera picked up his notation. He combined the two last names crossing out a few letters: "Randy-Navis = Randavis."

The unseen group of five exploded in laughter as he crumpled the paper, threw it to the floor in frustration, and abruptly left the lab. Paul, Julie, Nick, and Brenda thanked the young CIA agent who had delivered the balloon to Dr. Tompkins. The balloon had, of course, been covered with the agent's own saliva.

Brenda suddenly felt nauseous and made an abrupt departure. She couldn't believe how two months of marriage could leave her so tired and moody. She thought of swinging by the infirmary to have her temperature taken and get her blood pressure checked, but instead she shrugged it off as fatigue. After all, a lot had happened in the previous four months.

A few days later, Dr. Tompkins was elated to actually get a promotion! It was crafted to appeal to his vanity.

Dr. Tompkins,

In view of your honorable and sacrificial service to this country as an outstanding scientist, you have been selected to lead an elite group of scientists on a five-year study of the effects of global warming on arctic organisms.

Should you accept this presidential appointment, you are authorized to recruit any two trusted colleagues to join you. I personally deem this mission to be urgent and of utmost importance. Living conditions will at times be severe, but the future of human civilization on planet Earth may rest in your hands.

Please recognize that you have the full support of the Oval Office behind this appointment. Please contact me personally via my Oval Office hotline within 24 hours if you choose to accept this appointment.

Thank you,
The President of the United States of America

He gloated in self-pride as he held the document in his hands. At last he felt honored for all of his hard work. He was confident that even Julie would be jealous of his presidential appointment. He would flaunt it in front of her as he announced his regretful resignation from the research center. He lamented the fact that his choice of two loyal recruits from within the research center would undoubtedly spell the end of the secret society, but the rest of the group was falling apart regardless.

Besides, he now had more important matters calling for his expertise and previously unappreciated leadership. He also had something which he was sure would make Julie jealous. He had his promotion, signed directly by the president of the United States of America. Holding the document in his hand, he shouted out loud, "What vindication to know that I am known by name by the president of the United States while Dr. Julie Summers is nothing more than an obscure director of this research center."

Six months later, while huddled around a kerosene stove in a nylon tent on the frozen arctic tundra, he pointed to the framed document as indisputable proof to himself and his two recruits that their mission was of utmost importance. His pride and self-importance were not even daunted by the cold arctic blizzard that was now in its third consecutive week. Nor did the fact that it was the coldest winter on record affect his presuppositions of global warming, which he now referred to as "global climate change."

19

FINAL CONTAINMENT

With the absence of Dr. Tompkins, things around the research facility returned to normal. The two travel pods underwent radical modifications under the direction of Dr. Paul Summers and his younger understudy. By this time, the father-son team was inseparable.

Some of the technicians and scientists who had access to the control room argued against incorporating so many untested systems into the travel pods. The modifications represented technical leaps still years into the future, and it may actually have been easier to rebuild the pods from scratch than to modify them so extensively.

The antigravity propulsion systems took up a fraction of the space of the previous nuclear reactors. Very small but efficient nuclear generators were placed next to the antigravity mechanisms to supply power on demand. The previous battery and power storage units were removed completely and sent to the power plant at the research facility. One power storage unit had the capacity to run the entire facility for over ten years! It was hard to believe they arrived at the power plant with the words *Obsolete Technology* stamped on the side.

Pod #1 was converted into an advanced research lab. The front of the pod was retrofitted with what some surmised was some kind of galactic mining apparatus capable of collecting cosmic dust and particles then sorting and combining desired particles into raw materials and heavy metals. These were, in turn, stored in what Paul Summers and Nick Davis called "mega condensed gravity containers." These containers resembled miniature black holes and could literally store an entire solar system of condensed matter.

The galactic mining apparatus was also capable of detecting and dodging dark matter at near light speeds. The whole concept of dark matter was deemed by some to be theoretical, but the pod was being redesigned to go beyond theory.

Pod #2 was converted into living quarters. It too had a few mega condensed gravity containers that were dedicated to food storage. Ten trainloads of food and organic grains were condensed into one container no larger than a loaf of bread. Three of these containers were attached to the meal preparation module. In mere seconds, meals could be ordered, prepared, and served. It seemed obvious that the touch of human hands in the art of cooking and food preparation was about to be lost to advanced technology. Neither Brenda nor Julie complained as both lacked skills in the areas of food preparation and other homemaking tasks.

Pod #1 had a docking station added to one end while pod #2 had docking stations at both ends. This seemed odd to everyone at the research facility since there were only two known pods in existence and no plans in the works to build a third.

Another amazing thing was how fast work seemed to progress on the travel pods. It seemed to the technicians that years of labor were condensed into just days. It occurred to many at the research facility that not only was time being compressed but so too was space. For several weeks, trainload after trainload of supplies would arrive and be unloaded daily despite there being no increase in warehouse capacity. It was a mystery that no one tried to explain.

The only clock that seemed normal was the weekly growth of Dr. Brenda Randal Davis' belly. Her pregnancy was progressing at a normal pace, about three months ahead of Dr. Julie Summers', who by this time was also beginning to wear maternity clothes. The workload for the two had slowed considerably, mostly due to morning sickness. It was a condition they agreed warranted urgent research for a cure. Nick and Paul just smiled and promised that the cure would arrive within a few short months wrapped in maternity blankets.

No one at the facility even noticed the event on September 26 that brought a cataclysmic change to the research facility. Two beams of light flashed across the sky at precisely 1:00 p.m. There were no aftershocks or tremors. The control room had been sealed for what was termed a routine decontamination. The only anomaly was that it remained sealed for two full weeks. During that time, the four facility directors had also vanished from public view. The official report circulating around the facility was that both expectant mothers had taken maternity leave and had demanded that their husbands join them.

On October 7, a strong explosion rocked the research facility. It was nothing compared to the events of the previous year, but it was nonetheless of considerable concern to the geologists at the research facility. Two days later, Dr. Tompkins arrived at the facility accompanied by two Secret Service agents. He immediately called all department heads to the briefing room.

As they quietly filed into the conference room, Dr. Tompkins broke the silence by waving some papers in the air. He said, "These papers contain my appointment by the president of the United States as the new director of this facility. My authority is absolute, and my decisions are final. I have been briefed on the explosion that occurred on October 7 and have decided to take drastic measures to protect our environment." A few scientists tried to interrupt him and encourage him to look at the data, but he quickly cut them off.

He continued. "I have decided to launch Operation Blue Code as a precautionary measure to permanently seal the control room and contain any contamination. We cannot put the future of our planet or our environment at risk to unknown threats. Had I been in charge, this would have happened over a year ago! I just hope it's not too late."

The room erupted with objections from every department head. Many tried to get him to consider the loss of research, technology, and data that would accompany his rash decision. Several scientists lamented that it would literally push the clock backward to the dark ages of scientific knowledge. One scientist protested loudly, "For the sake of God and country, take time to think through your decision. We cannot long survive such atrocity."

Dr. Tompkins retorted, "From now on there will be no mention of any so-called 'God' at this facility. Religion is the enemy of truth, science, and research. The fate of mankind is exclusively in the hands of man." He decided to make an example of the outspoken scientist and had him forcibly removed from the meeting by two armed guards. It was obvious that guarding the principles of freedom of thought and speech were low on his list of priorities. The action brought temporary order to the meeting but did nothing to build respect or trust for the new research facility director—or dictator.

Two days later, in an attempt to prevent anarchy, Dr. Tompkins imposed a Code 1 Lockdown. Twelve hours later, the inner core of the research facility was shaken with a nuclear blast. The explosion was more severe than originally projected but successfully encased the control room, launch tunnels, and adjacent data center in the equivalent of thick glass. There were minor leaks of radiation but nothing else survived the blast. Dr. Tompkins congratulated himself that the system he had designed nearly a decade earlier had resulted in such a small environmental threat.

The decision reduced the facility to one-third its original size and research capacity. Over the next three months, many of the various department directors and staff accepted transfers to other government facilities or private-sector jobs. The new mission statement of the facility was displayed above the desk of Dr. Tompkins. It read: "Environment first; research, development, and progress last!" It was in bold print right under the two elegantly framed appointments from the president of the United States. Arranging and perfecting the display with just the right lighting became the new priority of the engineering department, second only to containing small, ongoing radiation leaks from Operation Blue Code.

Meanwhile, in a distant sector of the Milky Way Galaxy, four scientists were being briefed by the president of the United States via a giant screen in the living quarters of the three linked travel pods, while two infants engaged in playful research on the floor. The president spoke. "Your plan went forward without a hitch. I would say we now have 100 percent containment, thanks to the egotism of Dr. Tompkins." They all erupted into laughter. "Your mission now is to research the far sectors of the universe and to report back every few years."

There was a pause, and then three other people stepped into view behind the president. Tears blended with joy as the three proud parents bid a final farewell to their children, grandchildren, great-grandchild, and a very dear friend who still looked like a supermodel. Their family tree was confusing to say the least, but at last they had achieved containment. Before the screen when blank, the president's parting words were, "Do well for the sake of God and country. We will be praying for you."

In the pod, there was the daily practice of scripture reading and discussion. Topics often went down some very intellectually stimulating trails. The discussion on this day centered on instances of time and space manipulation alluded to as mysteries in the Bible—speculations on how both Moses and Elijah had appeared centuries after their time to meet and talk with Jesus on the Mount of Transfiguration. There were also discussions on how Jesus instantly turned water into wine and walked through solid walls with His glorified body after His resurrection. These four recognized that the Bible, rather than being a fictitious religious book, was light years ahead as a guide to scientific research and discoveries. It continually stretched and stimulated their creative imagination.

The day's discussion concluded at Nick's request. Paul chuckled and said, "Okay Dad, I guess you're ready for your first driving lesson."

At just that moment, a flash of light imploded into what resembled a tiny black hole, and the pods were gone. At least from this realm of time and space.

TRUTH QUEST: BONUS MATERIAL FOR THINKERS

The Bible urges Christians to "always be ready to give a defense to every-one who asks you a reason for the hope that is in you" (1 Peter 3:15). In Chapter Fifteen, Paul Summers confidently gave a logical defense of his faith to Dr. Tompkins. This bonus section is included for those of you who were challenged by the truths set forth in that chapter to go deeper and strengthen your own defense of the gospel. Enjoy your journey, and Godspeed!

Since the Book of Genesis in the Bible is the oldest reputable record of origins, let's analyze this account phrase by phrase.

"In the Beginning" (Genesis 1:1)

Every theory of origin recognizes a beginning, or an absolute starting point, for the physical matter in the universe. The first and second laws of thermodynamics point to an absolute starting point of all energy and matter. Albert Einstein's theory of relativity points to an absolute beginning.

The word *beginning* comes from the Greek Septuagint and does not accurately communicate the meaning of the Hebrew word *Bereshith*, used here originally. A better translation might be, "At the head, God created the heavens and the earth." This emphasizes more the event sequence and less the time sequence. Thus, Genesis 1:1 describes the beginning of events in the process of origin.

While there is generally no debate over the first three words of the Bible, the debate inevitably starts with the next two words of the Bible, "God created."

"God" (Genesis 1:1)

In a very real sense, time exists within God rather than God existing within time. God had already pre-existed for all eternity past before our dimension of time came into existence. But here God walks onto the stage of eternal nothingness and makes it clear that this is His story; He wants to be known. Hebrews 11:6 in the New Testament reads, "And without faith it is impossible to please Him, for he who comes to God must believe that He is, and that He is a rewarder of those who seek Him." Belief in the existence of God is an act of faith, but not blind faith. It is faith based on evidence. From the time God introduces Himself in Genesis 1:1, He begins to set forth the evidence of His own existence. Don't make the mistake of blindly arriving at a verdict until you have read and studied His case. Embracing atheism, or the belief that there is no God, without examining the evidence He set forth in the Bible is a leap of blind faith into nonbelief.

You may be wondering, So where did God come from? It has been said that God exists outside of the realm of time and space, and with the advent of extra-dimensional theories of reality within physics, this is conceivable. But technically time still applies to God. The time that applies to Him is eternity. He has been called the "Eternal Self-Existent One." Because He is spirit, God is not dependent on anything or anyone outside of Himself for His existence. Unlike people, God does not need air, food, or socialization to sustain life. According to the Bible, He always was and always will be. With this introduction in Genesis 1:1, God simply says, "I AM." Later in the Bible, He introduces Himself to Moses by that name (see Exodus 3:10–12).

The concept of eternality is hard to comprehend because human experience is packed with the temporary. Living organisms are born and they die. Material things are made and they rust or wear out. All things have shape and size and take up space. Experience teaches us that all things, including time, have a beginning and end. It is natural and automatic to superimpose human experience on our understanding of God, but this will only confuse the matter and lead to erroneous thoughts.

Questions such as Where did God come from? are natural questions and are flawed from the outset because they demand a natural answer. *When* and *where* questions relate to the natural realm of time and space. These questions force the supernatural into the box of natural understanding. Finite people will never understand the infinite God within the confines of human experience.

The amoeba in a test tube cannot comprehend the scientist who looks in from the outside unless the scientist finds a way to place evidence of him or herself within the test tube for the amoeba to examine. The weakness, of course, with this illustration is that both the amoeba and the scientist exist within the same dimension of time and space. So let's take a bigger step back and place the scientist in a completely different realm of time and space. Can you imagine the dilemma for the scientist when the amoeba says, "Unless I can experience you in my test tube, I simply will not believe you exist." Like the human atheist, the amoeba now becomes an "a-scientist" (not believing in the existence of a scientist), not because the scientist does not exist but rather because the test tube is too small or limited to contain the realm of the scientist. Unless the scientist can find a way to become another amoeba in the test tube, the amoeba might forever be an a-scientist.

"[God] Created" (Genesis 1:1)

Have you ever stood on a train track and watched a long train come towards you? Well, imagine this first verse in the Bible, Genesis 1:1, illustrated by a long freight train. At the head of the train is the powerful engine coming into view. As it approaches, the engine is seen and simply described as God. As the train passes through the pages of scripture, we see that there are actually three engines at the head of the train. The first engine is God the Father, Who planned the work of creation. The second engine is God the Son, Who performed the work of creation. The final engine is God the Holy Spirit, Who added order, design, and beauty to the work of creation. There were three inseparable engines working together at the head of the train. The cars behind the engine did not exist at the vantage point of Genesis 1:1, but the detailed blueprint and the energy or power needed for everything that followed was present and about to bring all else into existence.

Was the engine at the head strong enough to pull the train of origin into existence? Romans 1:20 in the New Testament says, "For since the creation of the world His invisible attributes, His eternal power and divine nature are clearly seen, being understood through what has been made so they are without excuse." The Bible opens with the existence of an eternal, intelligent, all-powerful being called God. He was at the head of what allowed or caused all that followed to happen. Whether you agree or disagree, you must acknowledge that the Bible presents an infinitely powerful cause to pull the train that followed.

Another question must also be asked: Is any cause less than the God of the Bible equal to the challenge of pulling the train of origin into existence? This is important because it separates the biblical equation of creation from all other equations, including atheistic evolution.

Consider the simple addition equation of factor plus factor equals sum (1+1=2). Let's assume that the first factor represents the existence or nonexistence of an all-powerful and intelligent being. (Existence is represented with a "B"; nonexistence is represented with a "0.") The second factor will represent the nonexistence of physical matter prior to it coming into existence. Compare the two equations and ask yourself, Which equation makes sense?

Evolution says: $0 + 0 = $ Everything

Creation says: $B + 0 = $ Everything

The most basic problem with the evolutionary equation is now obvious. Zero plus zero can equal nothing greater than zero. There is no way to work the equation and get a different or greater answer. Of course, the atheistic evolutionist would say the equation is not complete because the factors of time and random chance need to be added to the equation. I might frustrate the conversation by asking the question, Where did time come from? But let's skip that monumental problem for the sake of discussion. May I point out that the longer you work the equation of zero plus zero, the more convincing and certain the answer of zero becomes. Give it as many chances as you want for an infinite amount of time, and the answer is still zero. The first and most basic assumption of the atheistic evolutionary equation is now tragically clear and problematic.

It is at this point that I must raise an objection with my evolutionary friends who accuse me of committing intellectual suicide by believing in the Creation equation. May I point out that the Creation equation makes perfect mathematical sense the first time, and every time thereafter, that you work the equation. The sum or solution of the equation cannot be greater than one or a combination of both factors in the equation. If the God of Genesis 1:1 is removed from the equation of origin, there is nothing else that can be placed at the head of the train and yet have sufficient means or ability to pull the cars of physical matter, galactic order, and biological genetics into existence. Time and random chance are totally insufficient for the task. This is especially true when we consider that the train of reality consists of infinitely more cargo cars than physical matter, galactic order, and biological genetics. The Bible accurately opens with the phrase, "At the head, God."

To create is the first activity God performed, but it is insightful to list all the other activities attributed to God in the first thirty-four verses of the Bible (Genesis 1:1–2:3).

1.   God created. (Genesis 1:1)

2.   God moved. (Genesis 1:2)

3.   God said. (Genesis 1:3)

4.   God saw. (Genesis 1:4)

5.   God separated. (Genesis 1:4)

6.   God called. (Genesis 1:5)

7.   God made. (Genesis 1:7)

8.   God blessed. (Genesis 1:22)

9.   God completed. (Genesis 2:2)

10.   God rested. (Genesis 2:3)

When taken together, this list gives us a full and accurate picture of how God introduces Himself to mankind in the first chapter of the Bible. From these action verbs we understand the following about God: He is eternal. He is powerful. He is intelligent. He has personality and free will. This, of course, makes Him a person and not an impersonal force. He can see, think, evaluate, and communicate. He caused time, space, and physical matter to come into existence. This makes Him the Creator. He is also living. This makes Him the ultimate source of life. Notice that He also blessed what He made. This means that He is both caring and benevolent. Though not stated specifically, it can be inferred that He is also in control. Everything happened exactly as He planned. By the mere fact that He gave this introduction or revelation of Himself, we can also conclude that He is both knowable and wants to be known by His creation. This list of activities makes Him much more than the scientist in the previous illustration overlooking the amoeba in the test tube. He created both the test tube and the amoeba, plus He gave life to the amoeba. Surpassing the scientist, He is much more than an observer of what is; He is both the designer and cause of all that is.

This self-revelation of God also goes far beyond the theory that alien or extraterrestrial life forms from other parts of the galaxy or universe started the biosphere on Earth. The existence of other life forms elsewhere in the universe is another issue, but it falls far short of explaining the origin of the universe and physical matter.

"The Heavens and the Earth" (Genesis 1:1)

"We cannot leave verse 1 without observing what God made. He credits Himself with making both the heavens and earth out of nothing. The word *heavens* comes from the Hebrew words *shamayim* or *shameh*. These words arise from an unused Hebrew root, which primarily meant "to be lofty." These words are used many times in the Bible to describe the earth's atmosphere, the entire physical universe, and the spiritual realm. This may indicate that angelic beings were created at this time.

The word *earth* comes from the Hebrew word *erets* and simply refers to the planet Earth. When taken together, we discover that God's first act was to create all the physical matter in the universe from nothing that previously existed. This was the beginning of the three-dimensional realm of time, space, and substance. Not bad for one day's work!

The greatness of an artist is measured by his paintings. Buildings testify to the genius of the architect. So the greatness of God is measured by what He made. The grandeur and mystery of the universe is nothing compared to the grandeur and mystery of God. We, as people, through observation, try to discover what is and why and how it functions. When the subject of study is as immense as the universe, even the modern scientist assumes the role of the amoeba in the test tube.

"The Spirit of God Was Moving" (Genesis 1:2)

Notice that the second activity of God after creating the heavens and earth was to move. Genesis 2:2 says that God's Spirit moved over the formless void and darkness. Have you ever thought about the significance of motion in the process of origins? Technically, darkness is the absence of motion. Motion is energy. Energy times the speed of light squared, according to a simplified version of Einstein's theory of relativity, resulted in the formation of physical matter. However, Einstein failed to explain the source of energy needed to spark the process. Did the universe start with an uncaused Big Bang or did something cause the physical matter of the universe to come into existence?

The biblical answer is motion. The big question is who or what moved? According to the Bible, "God moved." How fast did God move? According to 1 John 1:5, "God is light and in Him there is no darkness at all." The motion of God's Spirit accelerated (or decelerated) to the speed of light, and in the process converted darkness into light and caused atoms to form. The laws of physics both predict and confirm much of this theory. In his attempt to explain the origin of the universe, Einstein almost climbed out of the test tube far enough to discover God.

"Then God Said, 'Let There Be Light'" (Genesis 1:3)

It is significant that the third activity of God is recorded in three words: "Then God said." Abstract words and speech are by-products of intelligence. God is pictured as speaking the blueprint of the physical universe into existence.

Many have tried to discredit the Genesis account of Creation with the question, How could there be light on the earth before the fourth day when God created the sun? With this question they insinuate a contradiction in the Creation account. The solution is given in the text. Simply stated, God's motion continued until He completed His work of Creation on the sixth day, and then He rested. Remember that motion is energy. When God rested on the seventh day, the completed universe with all the laws of physics took over and began to function in a state of maturity.

Are you ready for another illustration? During the first six days of Creation, the universe was like a fetus in the womb of God. In the Creation account, the womb was God's motion. In the development process of a baby, all the systems for life develop within the mother's womb and even begin to function. At the moment of birth, the new life begins to function and the mother enters into a time of rest from her pregnancy and delivery. This is a weak illustration, but it fits the description given in Genesis.

During the six days of Creation, the universe was formed within the womb of God's motion. It was literally engulfed in the energy of His light caused by motion. All the systems in the universe that are needed to support life were formed and began to function during this time frame. Even the genetic complexity of the biosphere was completed. When God rested on the seventh day, the birth of the universe was complete. Then, like the mother of a newborn healthy baby, God stood back and looked at all that He had made, and "behold it was good, it was very good." It was alive, and it was functioning on its own apart from the Creator. Though God involves Himself in the created realm, He exists separate and distinct from what He created. He exists apart from and beyond what He created.

"God Separated" (Genesis 1:4)

One of the most frequently repeated activities of God in the first chapter of the Bible is that He "separated." On the first day of Creation, all the raw physical matter in the universe was spoken into existence. Billions of atoms, a "formless void," became the building blocks with which God created. Everything that now exists, including all the interdependent systems in the universe, was separated and organized with order, design, complexity, and beauty according to His intelligent plan.

Then God Said, "Let the Earth Sprout Vegetation" (Genesis 1:11)

With the physical universe in place, God focused on the mystery of life and the biosphere. This presents a new problem because living organisms do not spontaneously generate from nonliving physical matter. Making the test tube was only the beginning; filling it with living amoebas represented a whole new challenge. The big question remains, Where did life come from?

If motion is energy, what is Spirit? Technically, Spirit is a giant step beyond energy. Spirit is life. Spirit must be added to the amino acids in the genetic code to make it come to life and start living. According to Genesis, all life has its origin in a living being called God. The laws of genetics and the specific genetic code for each kind or species of life were carefully assembled during this six-day time frame. The biblical account of Creation does not discredit microevolution within a species; it simply points to a separate creation or biological tree for each species of life.

Because the development of living organisms from inorganic matter is so statistically impossible by random chance alone, the atheistic scientist is forced to take a blind leap of faith and say it happened once. Then, because they cling to this one-time statistically impossible event, they are forced to explain how every species of life evolved from that living cell. They not only fail to explain how the first cell survived in a hostile environment, but they are also pressed to show how random chance guided that first cell into all the complexities of the biosphere. These are major problems when the God of Genesis is removed from the equation. The only answer is to add more time to the equation and hope for the best. In a moment we will discover that this creates a whole new problem.

"Bearing Fruit after Their Kind" (Genesis 1:11)

The Bible provides another explanation for the origin of species. The Intelligent Designer skipped all the intermediate steps and simply made all the separate species of life. From the outset He made a separate and unique genetic code for each species of life. The amino acid building blocks were the same, but the codes were different. From the start they began to live, function, and multiply after their kind. The result was a complete functioning biosphere with all the symbiotic relationships needed to sustain life.

Some argue that similar appearance and function in characteristic between different species point to a common origin of evolution. The theory of creation says it simply points to a common Designer.

The need for a complete functioning biosphere for any form of life to start and be sustained may explain why the billions of transitional life forms needed and predicted by the evolutionary model have never been found in the fossil record. Only those who reject an Intelligent Designer are compelled to keep searching for the imaginary transitional life forms that most likely never existed. Biased science books will forever be illustrated with pictures from science fiction artists rather than actual photographs.

"The Heavens and Earth Were Completed" (Genesis 2:1)

It is inconceivable that an incomplete solar system and biosphere could survive or function. Like in the case of a premature baby, the more premature the birth, the greater the likelihood of death. God had to bring the universe to a state of functioning maturity before resting, or it would not and could not have survived. Even theistic evolution, which states that God started the Big Bang and then traditional evolution took over, condemns the universe to a premature death. Time and random chance cannot complete what intelligent design began. Without the intervention of intelligent doctors and advanced life support equipment, premature babies do not have a chance. Factory workers do not begin the assembly process and then turn it over to random chance to complete the task. Random chance cannot read blueprints or follow detailed instructions.

Furthermore, there appears to be no independent or unnecessary functions in the universe. Though science has barely begun to unravel the mysteries of the universe, we see that everything functions together to allow the whole thing to work and exist. From the microscopic and atomic to the telescopic and galactic, it all fits and functions together as a whole. Though raw matter had a starting point, there was a gestational period needed to infuse it with order, form, and function according to an intelligent and infinitely complex plan.

Just like the body cannot survive apart from the heart, neither can the heart function without the body. The biosphere is also full of symbiotic relationships between living organisms that are dependent on each another for existence. It is not possible that all of these interdependent systems and organisms evolved as independent units and then further evolved into these interdependent relationships. Apart from their relationship to the mature functioning whole, they would not have purpose. In the same way, the human heart could not have evolved apart from the rest of the body. Apart from its relationship to the body, it has no purpose.

This is why the word *completed* is so important. Apart from completed, interdependent functioning systems, the source of energy that caused physical matter to come into existence could not rest. The universe would forever be dependent on the ongoing infusion of outside energy to feed the development process and keep the various wheels turning until the completed whole could take over and become self-generating.

This is where the billions of years required for evolution becomes a self-defeating problem. It's not enough to arbitrarily add more time to allow for random chance. You must also find a source to supply billions of years of sustaining energy to infuse into the undeveloped and nonfunctioning systems. Here is the problem; time is not energy. In fact, time consumes energy within the development process. The more time added to the equation in the developmental process, the more energy is wasted and consumed needlessly. The issue is not one of granting more time for evolution; the issue is one of finding the supply of more energy.

"God Rested" (Genesis 2:2)

According to the account of Creation as recorded in the Bible, God's creative motion lasted six days, and then He rested.

145

God infused energy into developing the interdependent systems of the universe for six days, and then it began to function and become self-sustaining. The universe may have been in an infant state, but all the systems including the biosphere were in a state of functional maturity. In other words, the gestational period for the creation of the universe within the womb of God's motion was six days, and then it was complete and ready to function on its own.

Some people reject the account of only six days because it sounds like a relatively short period of time. Keep in mind, the real question is: How long was the outside infusion of energy needed to bring the universe to the point of becoming self-generating and self-sustaining? The following comparison will be shocking. The six-day account of Creation is a very long period of time compared to the millisecond time period of the Big Bang Theory. If six days seems too short, how could a millisecond be more believable? This may sound like a contradiction to what I said in the previous paragraphs, but this is actually what evolution teaches. All the energy in the universe was infused in a millisecond during the Big Bang and has randomly been consumed over billions of years of developmental evolution by chance. Can you see the dilemma? There simply is not enough energy in the universe for the equation to work. Somehow, somewhere they need to find an outside supply for more energy. The concept of random chance over time in the development process is a poor manager of energy conservation.

The debate between creation and evolution is currently being waged in the arena of time. I believe this is the wrong arena. We need to think in terms of energy consumption over time. Thinking in these terms results in the following comparison. Creation teaches there's a long time for the infusion of energy (six days) and a relatively short time for the consumption of energy (thousands of years). By comparison, evolution teaches there's a short time for the infusion of energy (a millisecond) and an extremely long time for the consumption of energy (billions of years). Notice the vital difference. The equation of creation consumes infinitely less energy while infusing mega-volumes more. Meanwhile, the equation of evolution consumes infinitely more energy yet infuses mega-volumes less. Which formula makes more sense—having a huge supply with limited consumption, or limited supply with huge consumption? Let me ask it another way. Would you rather take a short trip with a full tank of gas or a long trip with a nearly empty tank of gas?

The Bible portrays the universe as a short trip with a full tank of gas. When God completed His work and rested on the seventh day, the creation of the whole universe was finished to the point of being self-sustaining and self-generating. Because God did not rest until the universe was mature and functioning, it appears to be much older than it actually is. He was the outside source of energy and intelligence that brought the whole universe to a state of functioning maturity.

What about those who claim the dates given in the Bible add up to around six thousand years? While it is true that Genesis 5 and 11 both give genealogy records, there is evidence within the Bible itself that the genealogical record and dates provided might be generally representative rather than specific. According to Jewish genealogical record-keeping practices, some generations may have been skipped over in the Genesis genealogies without compromising accuracy. For example, Luke chapter 3 includes at least one generation skipped in the Genesis account. I am, therefore, hesitant to assign an exact time frame because the Bible does not assign an exact time frame. However, the Bible clearly states that the engine that pulled the train of origin into existence pulled it all the way to completion, and it has been self-functioning in terms described by thousands, not millions or billions, of years.

Remember, this is God's story of how He claims things happened. If the biblical account is true, I would expect the universe to appear much older because the Bible states it was created in a state of functional maturity with the appearance of age. To a great extent, the billions of years needed for the standard evolutionary model is more driven philosophically than scientifically. When the engine at the head of the train is replaced with random chance over time, it just demands millions and even billions of years for mathematical glitches and mutations to produce the current paradox of precision, order, design, consistency, and detailed laws of physics and genetics that we observe in our present universe. It is an enigma how chance can produce detailed order and precise laws.

"Let Us Make Man in Our Image" (Genesis 1:26)

They are important words because they present the truth that God had a special place and purpose for people in His work of creation. According to the Bible, mankind did not evolve into the highest life form; rather, God directly created man as the crown of His creative work. The theory of evolution cannot explain the huge gap between other species of life and mankind. Animals are governed by instinct, and some can even think and do simple problem solving, but mankind, by contrast, can think in abstracts, communicate complex thoughts, and even invent tools and advanced technology.

I have watched the replay many times as the Apollo space mission put the first man on the surface of the moon. Televisions were wheeled into every classroom as the students watched live coverage of this historic event. It was a small step for a man, but a giant step for mankind. However, the animals were not entering into the celebration of this technological accomplishment. The birds were flying about and chirping, and the squirrels were gathering nuts and scampering up trees just as they had been doing for thousands of years with no conscious awareness of what happened on that day. It is more than egregious to note how far mankind had progressed with his ability to reason, design, invent, and develop technology.

Isn't it amazing that birds have wings, but it is mankind that has conquered the sky and reached the moon? For centuries, birds had the lead in the space program, but it wasn't because they were more intelligent or higher evolved than man; it was because they were designed to fly and that is what they have been doing for centuries. They haven't learned how to build winterized nests with heaters and running water, nor do they cultivate the ground and raise crops. Why haven't they invented oxygen tanks for high-altitude flying or sustained deep-sea diving? Why haven't they developed a school system to educate other birds in history, math, science, navigation, and linguistic skills? A little research and development would have secured their lead in the space race. Okay, I think you get my point, but why this huge gap between people and animals?

According to the Bible, God had a special purpose in creating man. Unlike the animals, only mankind was created in the image of God for the purpose of communication, relationship, and fellowship with Himself. God loves people and wants to reveal Himself to them, so He created man in His own image with the capacity for worship. Evolutionary thinking will never bridge the huge gap between man and animals, because God directly created you and me in His own image.

This has monumental implications for your life. You are neither a mutation nor a mistake. You have meaning, value, dignity, and purpose because God created you after His own likeness. You have been endowed with special gifts and abilities that no animal can match. As a human, you also have a calling on your life. This is where meaning, purpose, and direction in life come from. This calling is to enter into a personal relationship with God. The bottom line is that God loves you and wants to reveal Himself to you. This sounds wonderful, but there is a problem.

Every person has sinned and created a barrier between themselves and the God of creation. Genesis 3 includes the record of how Adam and Eve sinned and rebelled against God. Because of this event, which is commonly called "the Fall," all people became sinners, both by nature and by choice. Because of sin, fellowship with God was broken.

God is good, just, and holy. He will not allow sin into His presence. In the Old Testament, God gave the Ten Commandments to establish His standard of goodness. The problem is that no person has ever kept the Ten Commandments. People have rejected God, taken His name in vain, worshiped everything and anything in place of God, displaced Him as the Creator with the theory of evolution, dishonored their parents, killed, became immoral in thought or deed, stolen, lied, and coveted things to fill the void in their lives. These represent sin, and they drive a wedge between people and God.

Few of us have broken all of God's Commandments, but all of us have broken some. Just like it only takes one broken link in a chain for the whole chain to be broken, so it only takes one violation of the Ten Commandments for the whole law to be broken. Sin is falling short of God's glory as revealed in His law. It is disobedience to God.

This explains why so many people feel lost and separated from God with no meaning, purpose, or peace in life. The Bible teaches that we can become slaves of our own sinful ways making life miserable for others and ourselves. This is where all the pain and suffering in the world comes from. Mankind in his rebellion against God has created a world that reflects human depravity and the fallen nature of man. We need to be saved not only from our sin but also from ourselves.

How did something that started out so good end up so bad? Is there any hope? Fortunately, the rest of the Bible has some good news that you need to hear. "For God so loved the world, that He gave His only begotten Son, that whoever believes in Him should not perish but have everlasting life" (John 3:16).

God loves you so much that He sent his own Son to personally pay for your sins and remove your sin barrier. The mighty God who created the universe provided a way to forgive man of his sin and restore a basis of loving relationship and fellowship between Himself and sinful people. The solution was in His Son, Jesus Christ.

Because Jesus was conceived of the Virgin Mary, He did not have the sin nature, which is passed on through the male during conception. He was not a sinner by nature nor did He become a sinner through choice. He perfectly kept God's Law.

The Bible teaches in Romans 6:23 that "the wages of sin is death." Because Jesus was sinless, He did not have a death sentence on His life. He was immortal. Yet He died on the cross. Why? You are about to learn the most important truth in the whole Bible. Jesus loves you so much that He gave His life to pay for your sins. He became your substitute payment. He made provision to remove the sin barrier that separates you from God. Why did Jesus die in your place? Because He created you, and He loves you.

After His death on the cross, Jesus was put in a grave for three days. However, because of who He is, death could not hold Him. On the third day, Jesus rose from the dead and thereby proved that He was the Son of God. There are two basic things that separate Christianity from the world religions made by man. First, Christianity is a message of love, forgiveness, and the hope of a new life. Second, only Christianity validates the claims of its Founder through a factual historical resurrection.

"As many as receive Him, to them He gives the right to become children of God" (John 1:9). Jesus has done everything necessary for your sin barrier to be removed. He wants to forgive your sin, and He invites you into a wonderful relationship with Him, but He will not force Himself on anyone. In order to receive forgiveness of sin and the gift of eternal life, you must trust in, or receive, Jesus Christ as your personal Savior.

This is a big step. It involves confessing to God that you are a sinner and being willing to repent, or turn from your sinful ways. Becoming a Christian involves turning over the control of your life to God. How can you do this right now? In simple but sincere faith, talk to Jesus and ask Him to forgive your sins and become your Savior.

You may consider using the following prayer as a guide: "Dear Lord Jesus, I know that I am a sinner and that I need Your forgiveness. I believe that You died for my sins and that You paid my debt in full on the cross. I repent and confess my sins to You. Please forgive me and come into my heart and life as You said You would. I trust You as my Savior and follow You as my Lord. Thank You for answering my prayer."

Becoming a Christian is like becoming a new creation. God begins a work of change in your heart and life. Remember those activities of God recorded in the first two chapters of the Bible? The Holy Spirit will start doing some of those same kinds of things in your life. He will separate the light from the darkness and rearrange some things. Build your relationship with Him daily by reading the Bible and learn how to talk to Him through prayer.

God bless you!

Terry Baxter